KT-233-404

WITHDRAWN

X000 000 052 6364

ABERDEEN CITY LIBRARIES

A former au pair, bookseller, marketing manager and seafront trader, **Jessica Gilmore** now works for an environmental charity in York, England. Married with one daughter, one fluffy dog and two dog-loathing cats, she spends her time avoiding housework and can usually be found with her nose in a book. Jessica writes emotional romance with a hint of humour, a splash of sunshine and a great deal of delicious food—and equally delicious heroes!

Also by Jessica Gilmore

A Will, a Wish...a Proposal
Proposal at the Winter Ball
Her New Year Baby Secret
A Proposal from the Crown Prince
The Sheikh's Pregnant Bride
Baby Surprise for the Spanish Billionaire

The Life Swap miniseries

In the Boss's Castle
Unveiling the Bridesmaid

Discover more at millsandboon.co.uk.

SUMMER ROMANCE WITH THE ITALIAN TYCOON

JESSICA GILMORE

MILLS & BOON

All rights reserved including the right of reproduction
in whole or in part in any form. This edition is published
by arrangement with Harlequin Books S.A.

This is a work of fiction. Names, characters, places, locations
and incidents are purely fictional and bear no relationship to
any real life individuals, living or dead, or to any actual places,
business establishments, locations, events or incidents.
Any resemblance is entirely coincidental.

This book is sold subject to the condition that it shall not,
by way of trade or otherwise, be lent, resold, hired out
or otherwise circulated without the prior consent of the publisher
in any form of binding or cover other than that in which it is published
and without a similar condition including this condition
being imposed on the subsequent purchaser.

® and TM are trademarks owned and used by the trademark owner
and/or its licensee. Trademarks marked with ® are registered with the
United Kingdom Patent Office and/or the Office for Harmonisation
in the Internal Market and in other countries.

Published in Great Britain 2018
by Mills & Boon, an imprint of HarperCollins*Publishers*
1 London Bridge Street, London, SE1 9GF

© 2018 Jessica Gilmore

ISBN: 978-0-263-07640-0

MIX
Paper from
responsible sources
FSC® C007454

This book is produced from independently certified FSC™ paper
to ensure responsible forest management.
For more information visit www.harpercollins.co.uk/green.

Printed and bound in Great Britain
by CPI Group (UK) Ltd, Croydon, CR0 4YY

Thanks to everyone at Yorkshire Wildlife Trust for a lovely eight years—especially all the fabulous past and present members of the Development Team. Miss you all! xxx

CHAPTER ONE

MADELEINE PERCHED ON the edge of the small wooden jetty and slipped her bare feet into the cold lake, shivering at the first shock of icy water on her bare flesh. Cold as the glacier-fed lake remained despite the summer sun, the refreshing lap of waves against her hot feet usually soothed her, aided and abetted by the view. Even after nearly a year living in the Dolomites, the magnificent mountains soaring into the sky filled her with utter awe. The only thing marring her enjoyment of the landscape was the graceful castle on the other side of the lake, its delicate spires mirroring the mountain peaks. Madeleine was completely over admiring ancient, imposing seats of power; she much preferred the traditional chalets which populated San Tomo, the small village at the head of the lake.

But today she barely felt the water, hardly noticed the view. Pulling a crumpled envelope out of her pocket, she slipped the heavy cream card out of it and flipped it over, reading the engraved gold words yet again. Not that she actually needed to read it. By now she knew the brief contents off by heart.

Lady Navenby
requests the pleasure of the presence of

the Honourable Madeleine Fitzroy
at the wedding of her son,
Lord Theo Willoughby, Earl of Navenby,
and
Miss Elisaveta Marlowe
at Villa Rosa, L'Isola dei Fiori
31st August
RSVP to Flintock Hall

Madeleine turned the piece of card over and over, aware that she was frowning, her mother's voice echoing in her head warning her that she would get frown lines. What, she wondered, was the point of an expensive Swiss finishing school if she didn't know the correct etiquette when one was invited to one's ex-fiancé's wedding? Especially if one had made it all the way up the aisle and to the actual altar before said fiancé became an ex?

Not that she had any intention of actually *attending* this wedding. The last thing anyone really wanted was the groom's last bride-to-be hanging around like a modern-day Miss Havisham, the ghost of weddings past. But should she send a gift? If so, of what value? Theo and Elisaveta had her blessing, of course. After all, she was the one who had actually halted the wedding, right at the iconic 'Any persons here present' part.

No, it wasn't the happy couple that worried her. They belonged together in a way she and Theo never had. Madeleine stared down at her morose reflection in the water. She just hoped that this new wedding of Theo's, just a year after their own failed nuptials, wouldn't resurrect the intense and intrusive press interest in Madeleine herself.

Taking a deep breath, she tried to push the panic back down to where it usually lurked, never quite quelled but never acknowledged. She was safe here, far away from the British press and a scandal which surely most people had forgotten about. It had just been so unexpected. She'd never been a tabloid headline before—and fervently hoped she never would be again.

All she wanted was the whole mess to be forgotten. To move on. To be simply Maddie, no longer the Honourable Madeleine with all that entailed.

Speaking of which—she glanced at the watch on her wrist—'simply Maddie's' lunch break was nearly up. It took twenty minutes to walk around the small lake to the castle, where emails, to-do lists and myriad duties awaited her. Maddie shoved the envelope back into her pocket and scrambled to her feet, mentally calculating what she had to do that afternoon. Confirm numbers with the McKellans, finalise menu choices with the Wilsons and chat to the florist about the Shepherds' desire to only have buttercups and daisies in all their floral arrangements. The florist considered herself an artist and Maddie wasn't looking forward to conveying the bride's wishes and the ensuing conversation about the barbaric taste of the English.

Maddie was fully aware that it was more than a little ironic that a woman who had officially Had Enough of weddings *and* ancestral stately homes had secured a job combining both these elements. Yet here she was, wedding and event planner at Castello Falcone, ensuring the mainly British brides—and their grooms—had the perfect Italian wedding experience. At least she was getting a salary for her labour. The first money she had actually earned in her twenty-six years, as opposed to working all hours for love, board and an allowance. It was liberating, literally and metaphorically.

And by the end of the year, she would have enough money saved to head off somewhere where nobody had ever heard of the Honourable Runaway Bride.

Just one more moment. Maddie turned back to the mountains, raising her arms in a silent commune with the sun, with the landscape, with the heady fresh air. Closing her eyes, she basked in the sensual warmth of the sun on her face, the scent of pine. She stayed still for several seconds, arms still raised high, head tilted back until the sound of the church bell, dolefully ringing out the quarter-hour, reminded her that she really needed to be getting back. She lowered her arms and opened her eyes, only to freeze in place.

A man was getting undressed on the other side of the lake.

It wasn't a big lake, but long and skinny, the distance from one shore to the other widthways less than three hundred metres, perfectly swimmable if you didn't mind the cold. Which meant Maddie had a clear view of the small cove on the opposite shore and of the man purposefully and neatly divesting himself of trousers, of shirt, of socks and shoes until he stood there in just a pair of swim-shorts.

Look away, her conscience bade her. He was perfectly entitled to his swim, whoever he was. And she had places to be and many, many things to do. She certainly shouldn't be here ogling—because that, she guiltily admitted, was exactly what she was doing. Only she couldn't tear her gaze away.

He was tall and perfectly sculpted. Long, muscular legs led to a slim, defined torso which broadened out into a strong set of shoulders. Maddie could make out tousled dark hair, although his features were blurred. Unexpectedly desire hit her, hot and heavy, swirling low in her stomach, weakening her knees. Nostalgia followed, equally potent. It had been so long since she had experienced anything this intense. If ever.

'So you're reduced to gawping at half-naked strangers,' she muttered, half in self-disgust, half in self-deprecation as she made herself turn away. 'Face it, Maddie, this journey of discovery of yours is going to have to include getting back in the dating game. You want someone to really, passionately love you? They're going to have to get to know you first.'

Not that she *had* ever really dated. A series—a very short series—of monogamous, semi-serious relationships with suitable young men that she had eventually ended when she considered herself to be in real danger of dying from actual boredom, until she had allowed herself to get engaged to Theo Willoughby. Engaged even though he had never, not once, made her tremble with desire. Nor, she admitted, had she him. No wonder they'd both been content to drift through the two years of their engagement barely seeing each other—and barely touching when they did.

She took one last look back and stilled. The man was looking across at her, and even over the lake she could sense his predatory intenseness. Heat flickered through her veins as she stood there, trapped under the weight of his gaze, über-conscious of his semi-nudity, all that flesh so splendidly displayed, feeling, under the weight of his gaze, as if she were equally unclad. Her mouth dried, her limbs heavy, under his spell, as if he were some male Medusa, turning her into a statue with a look alone.

Somehow Maddie summoned up the resolve to turn away, to walk nonchalantly as if she didn't know that he was still staring at her, as if his gaze wasn't burning holes in her back. And then, just like that, the pressure lessened, and when she plucked up the courage to glance back he was in the water, cutting through the lake with single-minded, bold strokes.

She paused to watch him swim. She had no idea who he was, but the unsettling encounter combined with the wedding invitation had to be a sign. Theo had moved on—to be fair, he had moved on the second she had halted the wedding if not before—and it was time she shook off all those labels that had held her back for so long: dutiful daughter, the runaway bride, the Honourable Madeleine. It was time simply Maddie discovered the joys of falling in love as well as the joys of working for a living. She'd promised herself the chance to live, to have fun in this time of exploration. It was time she stopped hiding behind her work, behind her fear, and seized every opportunity.

Of course, there weren't that many opportunities for spontaneous romance in Castello Falcone or San Tomo, the tiny village which traditionally served the Falcone family. The pleasure spots of Lake Garda were twenty kilometres away, Verona and Milan further still. It was the peace and solitude which had drawn her here in the first place.

Lost in thought, Maddie barely noticed as she walked through the small, cobbled village square, with the church at one end and the magnificent wooden town hall at the other, passing through the narrow streets on autopilot. It wasn't until she found herself back on the lake path that Maddie realised that she'd missed the turning, which took her around the back of the castle and in through the discreet staff exit, and instead she was heading towards the much grander—and private—gated driveway. She stopped, irresolute. It would take longer for her to turn around and go the right way and it wasn't as if staff were actually forbidden from using the main entrance.

The fact this path would take her past the small cove where the mystery man was bathing had nothing to do with her decision to carry on. She focused on the path ahead, determined not to look to the right at any point, yet unable to stop her gaze sliding lakewards, just a little, as she approached the cove.

Nothing. No one. No piles of clothes. No bathers. Just a small curve of sand and the water.

That couldn't be disappointment tightening in her chest, could it? Because that would be ridiculous. If things had come to such a pass that voyeurism was how she was getting her admittedly very few kicks then maybe she should just admit defeat and start creating memes of kittens.

Putting her head down, Maddie trudged determinedly on, only to stop with a shocked gasp as she ran straight into something hard. Something that emitted an audible *'oof'* as her head rebounded off it. Maddie stepped back, embarrassed heat flooding her as she looked up, an apology spilling from her lips, only for the words to dry up as she looked into a pair of steely blue eyes. Eyes fixed directly on her.

'Trovi bella la veduta?' the owner of the eyes enquired sharply.

Maddie spoke fluent Italian, but every word she had

ever known deserted her. 'I... I'm sorry?' She cringed as
her words emerged, brisk and clear and so utterly English
she sounded like Lady Bracknell opining on handbags.

'I asked,' and she cringed further as the man switched
to perfect English, 'if you were enjoying the view?'

Oh, no—oh, absolutely no way was this happening.
Maddie stepped back and took in the man properly. Tall,
dark-haired, looked as if he was sporting a decent pair
of shoulders under the white linen shirt, hair ruffled and
still wet. Still wet...

The swimmer.

Dante raised an eyebrow, but the slim, blonde woman
didn't say anything further, fixing her gaze firmly on
the second button of his shirt. He raked her up and down
assessingly—tall, with a willowy grace when she wasn't
running into people—her long, silky blonde hair twisted
into a smooth ponytail. She didn't look like one of the
wedding guests who trooped through the castle gates
with clockwork regularity to swill Prosecco and party
into the early hours, rarely taking the time to notice the
exquisite setting, but who else could she be? So few tourists found their way to the small San Tomo lake, most
preferring the well-trodden loveliness of the more famous Garda and Como or to head deeper into the mountains.

The woman's pale cheeks flushed a deep rose-pink
as she finally lifted her head and met his gaze full-on.
Her own gaze was steady, strengthened by a pair of cool
grey eyes which reminded Dante of the lake on a winter's day; almost silver, tinged with a darkness that spoke
of hidden depths.

'I wasn't looking where I was going—please forgive me,' she said, her voice clear and bell-like.

'Distracted, maybe? The views can quite take one's breath away.' He allowed a knowing intonation to creep into his voice but, although her colour heightened, her expression stayed cool.

'The mountains are magnificent, aren't they? I can't imagine ever taking them for granted, ever not being overawed.'

'Glad to hear they've made an impression, *signorina…*' He paused and waited, watching her torn between good manners and reluctance to prolong the conversation.

'Fitzroy, Madeleine Fitzroy.' She smiled then, the kind of polite smile which was clearly a dismissal. 'I am so sorry again. It was nice to meet you.' And with that she turned and walked away, back along the path. A calm, collected walk as if she was not at all flustered. Dante stayed still for a moment, enjoying the sway of her hips, the curve of her waist, set off by her neat linen shift dress.

The ping of his phone reminded him of his duties. He couldn't stand here for ever, no matter how pretty the view. Tomorrow he would go for a long hike, up into the mountains, just as he had when he was a boy. But today he needed to catch up with paperwork, get to know any new staff who had started in the last few months, settle back into the castle after far too many months since his last fleeting visit.

The woman had disappeared around the curve of the lake path and Dante set off in the same direction. The path was as familiar as his own reflection, memories around every turn. Even now, after all these years, after all these regrets, he had to stop the moment Castello Falcone came fully into view. Had to admire the way the natural stream had been diverted to create a continuous cascade through fountains and ponds to fall down the terraced slopes. Appreciate how the natural and formal so seamlessly blended together in the landscaped gardens—and, rising above it all, the many spires of Castello Falcone. The setting was more fairy-tale than any movie-set designer could imagine, centuries of scandal and secrets locked up inside those walls. His own included.

His phone pinged again, this time telling him he had a call, and he pulled it from his pocket, frowning. He'd promised Arianna he'd try and take a break this summer, but he could never truly switch off. Too much rested on him. He flipped the phone over, his mood lightening when he saw his sister's name on the screen, mentally calculating the time difference. It must be midnight in New Zealand.

'*Ciao, Luciana. E tutto okay?*'

'Why wouldn't it be?'

Dante suppressed a smile at the familiar voice. After a decade on the other side of the world his sister had an accent that was a unique mixture of her native Italian and a New Zealand twang, and she usually spoke English, even to him, liberally strewn with Italian endearments and curses. His chest tightened. How he wished she were closer, were here to help him raise Arianna.

'It's late,' he pointed out mildly. 'I'm surprised to hear from you, that's all.'

'I just want to make sure that you're okay, *mio fratello*. Are you at the *castello*?'

'Arrived this morning,' Dante confirmed as he resumed his walk up the sweeping driveway, reaching one of the sets of stone steps flanking the terraces. 'Arianna's au pair will bring her along in a couple of days when I've made sure everything is ready.'

'Good; it's time she returned there. It's not healthy to keep away. For either of you.'

Dante did his best to bite back his curt reply, but the words escaped regardless. 'Her mother died thanks to the treacherous mountain roads. I was on the other side of the world. Arianna was left all alone...'

'The roads didn't kill Violetta,' his sister cut in. She knew her cue; after all, they'd had this conversation more times than Dante could remember. 'The mountains didn't kill her...not even the ice on the road was responsible. It was the driver of the car she was in. It was the drink and drugs. Arianna was safe enough with her nanny, with all the rest of the staff. Stop torturing yourself, Dante. It's been over five years.'

Over five years? What did years matter when the end result was the same? His daughter left motherless, his wife's death a dark stain on his soul.

'I know how long it's been, Ciana.' How long to the day, to the hour. Just as he knew how unhappy his wife had been. How, once she'd got over the initial excitement at living in a castle, she'd felt caged in by the mountains, isolated by San Tomo's remote location, how much she resented him for travelling so much, working so much—although that work paid for her extravagant lifestyle. That unhappiness, that resentment, that isolation had killed her—and Dante knew exactly who was to blame.

It wasn't the ice, or the car, or her lover, or the drink or the cocaine that had killed his wife. He had. And no matter how hard he worked he would never be able to atone, never make it up to his daughter. 'I'm fine, Luciana. Looking forward to spending the summer here. To getting away from Roma for a couple of months.' He glanced back towards the lake. 'I've already been for a swim.'

'The first swim of summer? How I miss it. I always knew it was the holidays as soon as I was in the lake. No study, no etiquette, no expectations for two whole months.' Luciana's voice was filled with melancholic nostalgia. Dante rolled his eyes, glad she couldn't see him. He knew full well his sister's house had stunning mountain views on every side, that she could walk down to a lake ten times the size of San Tomo in less than five minutes and her three sons spent most of their time on the water.

'There's plenty of room if you want to come for a visit any time.' The offer was genuinely meant, but Dante knew she was unlikely to make the two-day flight back to her native country any time soon, not with three boys aged between five and eight and the extensive vineyard she owned with her husband to manage.

'*Grazie*—it's been too long since I saw my niece. Now, Dante, I wanted to ask you a favour.'

Here it was, the reason for the call. 'Mmm?' he said noncommittally.

'My *amico*, Giovanna, you remember her? She recently got divorced—her husband was *not* a nice man— and she's moved to Milan. She could really do with a friend. Will you take her out? Maybe for dinner?' Luciana's voice was sly and Dante didn't try and hide his sigh.

'I'm not planning to spend any time in Milan this summer,' he said as repressively as possible. He should have known this conversation was coming; after all, it was at least three months since his sister had last tried to set him up.

'She has a villa on Lake Garda and spends all her weekends there. That's not far away. You could do with some time out as well, Dante. Just a few dinners, no expectations.'

'*Perdonami*, Luciana, but I'm not looking to make any new friends, to date anyone. I know you mean well, but please, stop trying to set me up with your friends.'

'I just hate to think of you all alone, brooding away.' Luciana sounded throaty, a hitch in her voice. Dante knew those signs all too well; his sister was going to cry.

It would be different if she was close by, if she could just see that he and Arianna were both well, both happy. But he knew how much she fretted about being on the other side of the world, how much she blamed herself for promoting Dante's marriage to Violetta. She just wanted him to be happy. How could he be upset with her for that? If only he could stop her worrying…

'I'm not alone…' The words spilled out before he had a chance to think what he was saying. 'I met someone, but it's really early days, so don't get excited.'

A little, teeny white lie. What harm could it do? If it made Luciana happy—and stopped her trying to set him up with any newly single friend then surely it was allowable? Maybe even the right thing to do.

'You met someone? Who? Oh, you *man*, you, why didn't you say something before?'

'It's not serious. I didn't want to get your hopes up.' Plus, the tiny point that he'd only just thought up his imaginary girlfriend.

'So? Details?' Luciana demanded and Dante stopped dead. Details? Of course his sister would want details.

He swivelled, looking out over the lake for inspiration. His gaze fell on the jetty almost directly opposite, on the woman he had seen standing there, on the intense way she had watched him, as if he represented something she needed, something she yearned for.

Despite himself the blood began to heat in his veins, his heart thumping a little louder. He'd been annoyed, sure. His coming-home ritual interrupted, the sheer intentness of her stare intrusive. And yet... There had been something almost sensual about the moment. The two of them separated by hundreds of metres of water and yet connected by something primal. He'd felt a little like a stag in the prime of his life, preening for attention. She the doe, unable to look away, waiting to be claimed.

'She's English,' Dante said slowly. 'Tall, blonde.'

'English? Okay. And? What does she do? Where did you meet? What does Arianna think?'

Dante seized on the last question gratefully, his inventiveness already giving out. 'Arianna doesn't know yet, so don't say anything when you video-call her. Like I said, it's early days. Luciana, I'll call you later this week; I have only been here a couple of hours and I need to meet the new staff and look over the new event planner's business plan.' Hopefully by then he would have thought up a story that would pass muster. Planned out a summer-long romance, followed by a regretful breakup in the autumn and his sister off his back for a good few months.

'Okay, but I want to know all about her,' Luciana threatened. *'Ciao, Dante.'*

'Ciao. And, Luciana? Thank you for calling. For always calling.'

'Stupido,' she murmured and hung up.

Dante slipped his phone back into his pocket, for once

the smile playing on his lips unforced. He did appreciate every phone call; he just wanted Luciana to stop worrying about him. Now, thanks to the stroke of genius that was his imaginary girlfriend, he'd achieved that.

For now.

CHAPTER TWO

'THAT'S GREAT. I look forward to meeting you in two weeks' time.' Madeleine replaced the phone handset and leaned back in her chair. There was no need for her to speak to Sally Capper again, but—she made a private bet with herself—there would be at least another four conversations before the bride arrived in San Tomo.

Of course, *every* bride put a lot of trust in Maddie's hands. She organised their pick-ups at the airport, she allocated rooms to their guests, sometimes ensuring that larger parties were also accommodated in the village. She arranged ceremonies at the church, at the town hall and in the small chapel in the *castello*—always reminding the couples to have a legal ceremony at home first to cut through the extensive Italian red tape. She advised on menus, she organised the decoration of the hall or the courtyard. She booked hairdressers and make-up artists. She received wedding dresses and made sure they were pressed and stored properly. In fact she had four hanging in the cedar closet behind her right now.

She soothed tears and tantrums, listened to diatribes about selfish relatives; she was counsellor and advisor. Some brides fell on her as if she were their best friend when they finally met. Others treated her as if she were there to do their every bidding, with no thought of pleases and thank-yous. Maddie didn't much care either way. She was here to do a job, that was all.

The truth was, most of the weddings left her cold, their very perfection unsettling. The only times she felt a glimmer of any emotion was when the bride and groom didn't care if the playlist was disrupted for a song or two, laughed if it rained, smiled benevolently when a great-uncle rose to his feet to make a long, rambling speech—because in the end all they cared about was each other. Maddie would watch those couples swaying later in the evening, eyes locked, and her heart would ache. Would anyone ever look at her that way—or would she always be practical, helpful Madeleine with the right name, the right upbringing and the right can-do attitude?

All she wanted was someone, some day to look at her as if she was their whole world.

Maybe she should get a dog.

She turned at the sound of voices in the courtyard behind her office. She'd waved off the last party yesterday and the rooms had all been cleaned and made up ready for the next, so no one should be out there. Maddie stood up to see better, but couldn't see anybody.

Stretching, she snapped her laptop shut, deciding she wasn't going to get much more done today; another wedding party would be arriving tomorrow and the exhausting cycle would begin again. Technically she was supposed to take the two days between bookings off, but she rarely did. There would be plenty of time for leisure and adventure when she finally had enough saved to begin travelling properly.

Picking up her bag, she stepped over to the little oval door which took her onto the covered balcony walkway with stone steps leading down into the courtyard. Her office was at the very back of the castle, overlooking the beautiful, cobbled courtyard with its gracious arches, flower-filled pots and imposing marble fountain which marked the centre.

Madeleine had been offered a room in the castle, but she had taken a small apartment in a chalet on the out-skirts of the village. She had grown up surrounded by the old and grand at Stilling Abbey. She knew all about graceful arches and medieval halls and battlements. About draughty corridors and smoking chimneys, about slippery, steep stone steps and tiny windows which let in hardly any light. About furniture older than most people could trace back their family trees and dirty oil paintings featuring disapproving-looking ancestors.

No. Let the brides and grooms exclaim over the ro-mance of it all from their four-poster bed while she went home to her little one-bedroom apartment with its glori-ous view of the lakes and its humble furnishings chosen for comfort alone. There wasn't a single antique, noth-ing worth more than a handful of euros in the apart-ment, and Maddie liked it that way, although she knew her mother would wince at the clashing bright colours of the throws and cushions with which Maddie had per-sonalised her little home.

She started down the old stone steps, mentally totting up all the things she needed to do the next day, not reg-istering the small group in the corner of the courtyard until she reached the ground. The sound of her heels on the cobbles must have advertised her presence because the three men all stopped talking and turned as one. Maddie paused, smiling automatically, registering her boss, the castle general manager, Guido, and an older man she recognised as one of the accountants from the Falcone headquarters in Rome.

Her heart stuttered to a stop as her gaze moved on to the third man. What was the bather from the lake doing here? By the flare in his blue eyes he was as surprised to see her as she him—but then, it was a tiny valley, one small village, where everyone knew each other. The chances of the mystery man not being connected with the castle were far less than running into him.

After the first flare of surprise his expression smoothed into neutrality as he stepped forward. 'Nice to meet you again, *signorina*.'

Guido looked from one to another. 'You know one another?'

'We ran into each other at the lake, but we haven't been formally introduced,' he said.

Maddie clenched her fists at the mocking tone in his voice, but managed to twist her mouth into a smile. 'Literally ran into each other. My fault.'

'I believe the *signorina* was transfixed by the view.'

Maddie's fists tightened as her smile widened. 'My mind was elsewhere,' she agreed, trying her best not to let him see how easily he riled her.

'Maddie is one of our hardest workers. We are very lucky to have her.' Guido stepped in, to Maddie's profound relief. 'Dante, this is Madeleine Fitzroy; she looks after all the weddings here at the *castello*. Maddie, let me introduce you to Conte Falcone.'

Maddie had already started to extend her hand and continued the motion automatically, even as her mind raced with the new information. It wasn't the dark-haired man's title that threw her—most of Maddie's family had titles—it was the realisation that he was her employer.

The first employer she had ever had and he'd seen her ogling him down at the lake. Was that an automatic disciplinary?

'You're the events planner?' He sounded as surprised as Maddie felt as he took her hand. It was just a brief touch, but a jolt shocked up and down her arm, her nerves tingling from the encounter.

'I...yes. I...'

Nicely done, Maddie; pull yourself together.

After all, she'd had tea with the Queen three times and managed to make polite conversation over the finger sandwiches just fine. There was no way this tall man with the sardonic smile was more intimidating than meeting the Queen of England. 'I've been here nearly a year now; I started last September.' A couple of months after her non-wedding, desperate to get away from the limelight she had found herself in, away from the camera lenses and the headlines, from her mother's disapproving and palpable disappointment. A friend of a friend had mentioned that she knew of a job somewhere remote in the Italian Dolomites for someone with good organisational skills and fluent Italian, and Maddie had jumped at the opportunity.

'You approved her appointment before you went back to Roma at the end of last summer,' Guido said. 'Maddie managed events at two similar venues in England.'

So her CV had carefully omitted that one of those venues was her own ancestral home and the other belonged to her ex-fiancé? The blatant nepotism and lack of a salary didn't change the fact that Maddie had managed them both expertly, and she had had no qualms about using that experience to get herself a real paying job.

'*Si*, I remember. I was expecting someone a little

older, that is all. I seem to remember at least eight years' experience at the highest level…'

'I started working young,' Maddie said, lifting her bag higher onto her shoulder, signalling clearly that, lovely as this encounter was, she had somewhere else to be.

'Obviously.' His smile didn't reach his eyes and Maddie shifted, uncomfortable with the scrutiny.

'Are you in a hurry?' Guido asked her. 'I was planning to show the Conte some of the changes you have made to the accommodation. But you can explain your thinking much better than I can, if you have time to accompany us.'

Maddie shifted again. Usually she would jump at the opportunity to showcase some of her work; she was proud of what she had achieved over the last few months. But she felt uneasy spending any more time under Dante Falcone's all too penetrating glance.

'I'm sure the *signorina* has more inspiring things to do with her evening; a walk around the lake perhaps?' the Conte drawled, his eyes gleaming at her.

Maddie tilted her chin defiantly. 'Of course I'd be glad to show you around. If you'd like to follow me?'

Maddie's job revolved in and around the courtyard. The top two storeys of the old stables which made up two sides of the rectangle had been converted into guest accommodation, comfortably housing around sixty guests in comfortable en-suite bedrooms. The ground floor of one block was fitted out with a sitting room, a library and a games room, whilst the other block was home to the large dining room serving breakfasts and dinners throughout the week, as well as a drying room for walking boots or skis for the more adventurous wedding guests.

The oldest part of the castle made up the third side of the quad. The medieval hall was often used for the wedding ceremony and reception, although in summer some guests preferred to hold the wedding al fresco. That was just one of the innovations Maddie had brought in when she had been appointed.

Now she had to impress the Conte with the rest. Let him mock. Bookings were up and referrals at an all-time high. Her record spoke for itself.

Maddie led the way into the grey flagstone entrance hall which linked the two stable blocks and paused by the comfortable leather sofas, cushions plumped up perfectly to welcome weary revellers. A coffee table between them was heaped with crisp new magazines and literature detailing walks and day trips. The sideboard held jugs of fresh mountain flowers and a chalkboard was propped against the wall opposite, the names *'Tom and Nicky'* written in a swirly script, ready to welcome the next happy couple.

'Although the *castello* is very beautiful, and architecturally sound, bookings were a little more intermittent than I would have expected,' she explained, proud of how firm her voice was. But why shouldn't it be? She had this.

'This is why I wanted a dedicated wedding planner,' Guido said. 'We got many enquiries, but only a few converted into bookings. We are so remote here, and the winters can be harsh, so our summers were busy but the rest of the year not so much.'

'It's just a case of turning those perceived negatives into positives,' Maddie said. 'Positioning the castle as a winter wonderland through the colder months, making the isolation a strength by ensuring everything they could possibly need is right here, although we can organise trips to Garda or Verona or Milan. We organise airport pick-ups, help brides and their guests with travel itineraries either side of their stay with us.'

She opened the door that led into the dining room. The wooden tables were set out café-style, each with small jugs of fresh flowers in the centre. 'There is always coffee on the go in here, along with iced water, but guests can order any other drinks they need from the kitchens. Depending on the arrangements we have with the bride and groom, this might be free, or the guests might have individual tabs. We usually have some kind of cake or biscuits and bowls of fresh fruit available all day as well. Breakfast is always served as a buffet, dinner too unless the couple pay more for a more formal serving.'

Maddie was aware of the Conte's gaze, fixed firmly on her as she talked, but she blocked it out, determined that by the time her tour was concluded that sardonic gleam would turn to interest and the only expression on his admittedly handsome face would be approval.

Dante had to admit that the English girl had done wonders. The last time he had seen these rooms they had been furnished formally, antiques from the castle forming the bulk of the furniture, ancient mountain views and various ancestors framed in thick gilt decorating the walls. It had all been stripped away, plain white walls now livened with colourful abstract prints, and rooms filled with comfortable-looking brown leather sofas and chairs, heaped with bright throws and cushions. Shelving had been erected in both rooms, filled with books and board games. It looked clean, comfortable and homely, despite the size of the rooms.

The same magic had been wrought upstairs. The bedrooms were also freshly painted in white, the wooden beds made up with white linen and cheerful silk cushions and throws, with matching rugs on the polished floorboards. 'Sometimes a bride and groom like to decorate to a theme, so we've kept the accommodation neutral in case we need to dress the rooms up to match,' Maddie explained. 'There are still some of the castle antiques around—that huge vase, for example, but they're accents now, not overshadowing the whole. What we haven't stinted on is quality. All the toiletries, the linens, the chocolates are locally sourced. We want the stables to feel more like a high-end hotel, not like a hostel. All the rooms are Austrian twins so we can make them up as twins or doubles, depending on what we're asked to do.'

'It's very impressive,' Dante admitted as they reached the final room on that corridor, a sunlit room with cheerful yellow and orange hints. It was, and he especially liked how Maddie had managed to ensure that no two rooms felt the same, her judicious use of pictures and ornaments giving each one its own identity. 'But new sofas, new beds, new linen—it can't have been cheap.'

Not that he couldn't afford it, but the wedding lets were just a tiny part of his business concerns. The Falcone fortune came from agriculture, from shipping, from olives and wine. He was glad the castle was more than a glorified summer residence, glad to provide legitimate employment for those villagers who needed it, but he wasn't running a charity and the Castello Falcone needed to pay its way.

'It wasn't. But I believe the results speak for themselves. We're already fully booked for next year and a third of the year after, and we managed to fill every spare week this year from April onwards.' Maddie met his eyes with a cool gaze of her own, but Dante could see a swirl of uncertainty behind the grey depths.

'Impressive,' he said softly and watched, fascinated, as the uncertainty dissolved, her eyes lightening to silver, her diffidence disappearing until she was glowing with achievement and pride—deservedly so.

The air stilled, thickened as their gazes locked. Guido and Toni, his accountant, had returned downstairs to look at something that needed replacing, leaving Dante alone with his new event planner. And suddenly that felt like a dangerous place to be.

This was his home, his workplace—and more importantly his daughter was arriving in two days. There was no time for a discreet affair, even if Maddie was interested.

No, better not to think about an interested Maddie, not with the two of them alone, with her eyes still fixed on his, her lips parted. Not with the memory of how she had watched him across the lake still crystal-clear in his mind.

'I think that's everything,' she said a little huskily, colour mounting in her cheeks as she practically marched out of the bedroom and headed towards the stairs. 'I'm sure Guido has already talked you through the strategy we put together.'

'Have you also made changes to the master bedroom suite?' Dante stayed as still a predator as Maddie stopped, one hand on the top of the stair rail.

'A few.'

'Show me.'

Her eyes flashed at the order, but she didn't speak, just nodded her head slightly before descending the narrow staircase. Dante followed, trying not to watch the sway of her hips, the way her hair moved as she walked. If he had any sense he would allow Madeleine Fitzroy to get on with her evening and check out the honeymoon suite by himself. After another dip in the freezing lake.

Not that he had any interest in spending more time with Maddie. This was business, plain and simple. If she had made changes it made sense that she was the one to explain her rationale to him. His decision was completely unconnected to the knowledge that ever since he had seen her across the lake staring at him with such unabashed curiosity something dormant had woken inside him, running insistently through his blood. Not because describing his fake relationship to his sister had made him aware of just how cold his life really was.

Intentionally cold, but when loneliness bit it did so with sharp intent.

It only took a few moments to cross the courtyard to the big, arched wooden door studded with iron which led into the oldest part of the castle. The wing where the staff quarters and offices were sat at a right angle to the ancient hall, with the more modern parts of the castle—a mere five hundred years old—complete with the famed turrets and terraces, faced the lake beyond that.

'I changed nothing in here,' Maddie said quietly as she preceded Dante into the vast room. 'It's perfect as it is.'

It was, with its arched ceiling criss-crossed with beams, the stone floor and the leaded stained-glass windows shadowing the floor in colour. A dais stood at one end filled with flowers. Chairs were already laid out in neat rows, each one dressed in white linen, more flowers punctuating the end of each row on tall plinths.

'Tomorrow's couple are getting married the day after they arrive, so we're all set up and ready,' she said.

Dante watched her as she stopped and surveyed the room, her sharp gaze sweeping every corner, making sure nothing was missed, pulling a notebook out of her bag and scribbling a few words. It was like watching a dance, or listening to finely read poetry, she was so in tune with her surroundings, oblivious to her companion as she wrote, paced a few steps, frowned and wrote again. Dante wasn't used to being forgotten, especially by women. It was a novel sensation—and it brought out a deeply buried, animal wish to make her notice him, the way a bird must feel as he preened to attract a mate.

He pulled out his phone and began to scroll through his messages, ruthlessly clamping down on any animal instincts.

'Sorry, I just noticed a couple of things.' Maddie put the notebook back in her bag and gestured towards the spiral staircase at the end of the hall. 'Shall we?'

'Of course.'

The staircase led directly into the honeymoon suite. Last time Dante had set foot in it, it had been a dark, richly decorated suite of rooms, little light able to penetrate the stone walls through the window slits. Ancient tapestries had hung on the walls, the flagstones covered with antique rugs, and dark, heavy furniture had dominated the space. It had felt baronial, grand and imposing—more like the lair of a medieval seducer than a romantic getaway.

He stopped as he reached the top of the room and swivelled, unable to believe his eyes. How could this be the same space? 'Where have the walls gone?' he managed to say eventually.

'They weren't original, don't worry. In fact they weren't even Renaissance like the rest of the castle, but a nineteenth-century addition, according to the architect I consulted,' Maddie said hurriedly, her gaze fixed anxiously on him. 'What do you think?'

The apartment was now one huge room, much lighter thanks to the clever use of mirrors picking up the faint light and reflecting it back into the room. The same imposing four-poster—a bed that legend had it Dante's great-grandfather times several greats had used to seduce women away from their husbands, until he had foolishly turned his wandering eye on a Borgia wife—was still in situ, but, placed at one end of the room and heaped with cushions, it looked inviting rather than intimidating. The matching wardrobe and chest of drawers also looked more fitting, now they no longer dominated the space.

The fireplace had been opened out and was, despite the summer's day, filled with logs ready to be lit. A comfortable chaise, loveseat and sofa were grouped around it. A small dining table, already laid for two, sat on one side of the room, low bookshelves lay opposite it and thick rugs covered the cold stone floor.

Dante stood stock still, taking it all in. How could such a dark, stately space feel so welcoming just because a couple of walls had been removed?

It wasn't just the walls though. It was the mirrors, it was the choice of painting, the cream rugs with the hint of gold, the dainty china on the table, the...hang on, the *what*?

'Why is the bathtub in the middle of the room?' Dante blinked again, but sure enough it was still there. Mounted on a tiled dais, the antique cast-iron bath that had used to reside in the bathroom now sat slap bang in the middle of the room. A freestanding wooden towel rail stood on one side; a slender console table on the other held candles and bath oils.

'We turned the bathroom into a wet room.' Maddie glanced at him, long eyelashes shielding her expression. 'Guido offered to email you the plans, but you said you trusted us to do the details.'

'Si.' Dante was still transfixed by the bathtub. Noting how it was in every possible eye line. How a man could lie in bed and watch his bride bathe, the candlelight casting a warm glow over her skin. 'And this is the kind of detail you like? The idea of watching someone bathe?'

'I…' She stopped.

Dante waited, lounging against the wall, eyes fixed on her as intently as hers had been fixed on him.

'Many luxury rooms have the bath in the main space.' Maddie turned away, but Dante had already spotted the red on her cheeks, on her neck. 'It's nothing new.'

'I'm quite aware of that,' Dante said silkily. 'It can definitely add a certain intimacy to an evening.' He deliberately took his time over the word 'intimacy', drawing out every letter as he spoke. 'That's not what I asked, Madeleine. I asked if you like to watch people bathe.'

'I…' she began again, then paused, before turning and determinedly fixing her gaze on his, head high, as proud as a young goddess. 'I owe you an apology. I intruded on a private moment earlier today and I…' She paused again, her eyes darkening. Dante watched, fascinated.

'No, actually I don't apologise,' she said, head even higher. 'You were bathing on a public beach—anyone could have seen you. If anyone should apologise, you should for trying to embarrass me.'

Dante stayed stock still, torn between amusement at her indignation—and shame. She was right; he *was* trying to embarrass her. Why? Because of the thrill that had shot through him when he noticed her watching him, had realised how enthralled she was, how safe it had been to retaliate, to look back with a lake between them?

He was her employer, had power over her. It was beneath him to indulge in these kinds of games.

'*Mi scusa*, you are right. It was wrong of me. It won't happen again. Thank you for your tour, *signorina*; enjoy your evening.' With a nod of his head Dante turned and left, vowing as he did so to keep every interaction with Madeleine Fitzroy professional and brief. They might be sharing the *castello* for the rest of the summer, but it was a big space. There was really no need for them to interact at all.

CHAPTER THREE

DANTE LOOKED OUT of the window. The lake was calm, the sun reflecting off it in myriad dancing sparkles, the mountains rising behind in a majestic semicircle. His chest tightened with the all too familiar mixture of longing and loathing. Once the *castello* had been his home, the place he loved more than any other. Now it was a constant reminder of his marriage. His greatest failure.

He resolutely turned back to his computer screen, but as he did so his gaze fell on the framed photo on his desk; a black and white portrait of a young woman cradling a baby. Violetta with a newly born Arianna.

If Dante had had his way all pictures of Violetta would have been destroyed the day after her funeral, but he knew that their daughter needed to grow up seeing her mother around her house, to know her face, to hear her name spoken. So he had gritted his teeth and kept Violetta's photos and portraits on walls and desks in Rome and here in the *castello*—and if he felt the bitterness of guilt and self-loathing each time he saw her face then wasn't it simply what he deserved?

He couldn't regret a marriage which had brought him his daughter, but he could excoriate himself for being the kind of fool to fall for a beautiful face and to project his own hopes and dreams into the woman who wore it. If he'd been older, wiser, had actually bothered to look behind the mask, then he would have seen that all Violetta wanted was the title and the *castello*—and the second of those had palled soon enough. She was bored, he worked too hard, was away too much. He thought motherhood might soothe and focus her. He'd been tragically wrong.

Wrong and blind. Too caught up in his own narrative. He'd never make that mistake again. How could he trust himself when love had proved nothing but a lie? Violetta had loved the title. He had loved a façade.

The tragedy was he had really fallen hard for that façade. Loved it truly and sincerely. Part of him mourned it still.

'*Al diavolo,*' he muttered. It was a beautiful summer's day; somewhere in the *castello* grounds his daughter was playing. Work could wait, especially on a weekend. He'd learned that lesson at last. But as he pushed his chair back his computer flashed up a video-call alert. Dante hovered, uncertainly, before lowering himself reluctantly into his seat and pressing 'accept'. Only a few people had his details. It must be important.

'*Ciao!*'

Dante leaned back as the screen filled with his sister's beaming face. Luciana was ageless, five years older than him, mother of three, but no wrinkles marred her olive skin, her hair as dark and lustrous as it had ever been. Only her eyes, he noted, seemed dull with fatigue, her smile maybe a little more forced than usual. 'Twice in one week. To what do I owe the pleasure?'

'Is that any way to greet your only sister?' Luciana asked, not giving him time to answer. 'Where's my niece? Did she arrive safely?'

'She's out playing and yes, she's already familiarised herself with every corner, just like we used to do.' Luciana and Dante had been heartbroken when their parents moved from the castle to the austere townhouse in Milan when Luciana hit her teens. Dante had sworn then that when *he* was the Conte he would never live anywhere else.

For four years he hadn't. He'd thought they were happy years. Had he been wilfully blind or simply ignorant?

'And? How are things with your mystery girlfriend?' Luciana's gaze sharpened. 'Did you tell me her name?'

Of course he hadn't—and Dante knew his sister was fully aware of that fact. 'I don't believe so.' He sat back even further, legs outstretched, grinning as his sister narrowed her eyes at him.

'Dante, don't be tiresome.'

'Early days, remember?'

'*Si*, I know. But I've been so worried about you, *mio fratello*, I just want to share in your happiness that's all. Tell me a little about her, about how you met.'

Damn. Now what was he supposed to do? He'd never been very good at this kind of thing even when the object of his supposed affections wasn't made up. Dante glanced towards the lake, hoping for inspiration. A group of young people, armed with kayaks and paddleboards, were on the beach just outside the castle gates—probably wedding guests. Guido mentioned that Maddie had introduced water sports for the summer months.

Maddie. Of course. He had already based his fictional girlfriend on her physically. What harm in borrowing a little bit more?

Crossing his fingers, he attempted a casual tone. 'She

works here at the Castello Falcone. I met her when we had a planning meeting last month.'

'*And?*'

'And what?'

'Did you like her immediately? Was there chemistry?'

Dante thought back to the moment when he had glimpsed Maddie across the lake, gazes holding, blood thundering. To the way he had been aware of every inch of Madeleine while she showed him around the stable block, the way he had tried to get under her skin, repayment for the way she seemed to get under his. The way he had assiduously avoided every place she might be in the three days since they'd met, working from the office in his suite of rooms in the main part of the castle instead of setting up in the main offices at the back as he usually would. 'I don't know about like,' he said slowly. 'But there was definitely chemistry.'

'And now you'll be working together all summer! Just promise me, Dante, don't try and sabotage this out of some ridiculous sense of loyalty to Violetta. It's been five years. It's time to move on.'

Dante didn't answer. He *had* moved on, but he had learned his lesson; his heart couldn't be trusted. If he was ever to consider marriage again it would be to someone practical, someone who could help him run his business empire and wouldn't be overawed by the social demands his title still commanded even in republican modern-day Italy.

'So you met, there was chemistry and now you and… what's her name, did you say?'

Dante knew when he was beat. 'Madeleine. Maddie.'

'Now you and Madeleine get to spend the summer together. It couldn't be more perfect. I can't wait to meet her.'

Hang on, *what*? 'Meet her?'

'*Si*; oh, silly me, that's the whole reason for the call. I've been so tired, Dante, not at all like myself—Phil even made me go and see the doctor, ridiculous, overbearing man.' Luciana's voice softened as she said her husband's name, just as it always did.

Dread stole over Dante's heart. He hadn't been imagining the dullness in Luciana's eyes, the shadows darkening them. 'Is everything okay?'

'Apart from having a dozen tests and goodness knows how many needles stuck in me? *Si*. At least, the doctor wants me to slow down for a while, but nothing worse than that. But how can I, with the boys and the vineyard and my fundraising and everything else I have to do? The truth is I'm just run-down. So Phil is insisting I take a good, long vacation. That I come home for a few weeks and let the Italian air revive me.'

'You're coming here? To San Tomo?'

'Isn't it wonderful?'

'Yes.' And it was. Of course it was. If only he hadn't just lied to her.

'I thought I'd spend a few days with you and then head to Lucerne to see Mama. I can get to know Arianna properly all over again and meet your Madeleine, plus get away from this dreary winter. My flight leaves in three days, via a stopover in Singapore. I'll be with you on Thursday!'

'Thursday?' Dante mechanically took down his sister's flight details, promising someone would be there at the airport to pick her up; all the while his brain was whirling, trying to work out a plan. Luciana would land in Rome in less than a week. She may choose to spend a few days in the apartment she had inherited from their father there, but knowing his sister she would be straight onto the high-speed train which would whisk her up to the north of the country in a matter of hours.

He had four days to work out a plan.

Maybe he could say his girlfriend had had to return to England?

Only he had not only named her and described her, but he had also given the name and description of someone here in the *castello*.

Maybe he could send Maddie back to the UK for a few weeks—or to his Rome office or Milan?

Only she had a summer's worth of weddings lined up and ready to go.

He could admit the truth. Break his sister's heart in the process—and find himself dating half of her friends in order to make it up to her.

He was in trouble whatever he did.

Unless…

Maybe, just maybe, he could salvage this situation after all.

Maddie hadn't felt like taking her usual lunchtime walks around the lake over the last few days. Her whole body still flushed when she thought about the moment she realised that her mystery bather and the Conte Falcone were one and the same—and when she remembered the peculiarly charged feeling permeating the air when he'd turned his whole focus onto her.

Instead Maddie had been exploring the vast gardens at the back of the castle. The formal walled gardens and flower gardens gave way to woodland and there were plenty of paths to wander through, plenty of interesting sights to discover, from little stone summer houses to statues, all relics of a nineteenth-century Falcone with a taste for whimsy. She had a similar ancestor; he had installed a gothic folly by the Capability Brown designed lake. It was a popular wedding spot now, which probably made her Byron-idolising ancestor turn in his equally gothic grave.

Maddie stopped when she reached the carved stone bench she'd discovered yesterday, sitting down in the pretty flower-strewn glade to eat the small picnic lunch she carried with her. She'd soon learned that if she didn't leave her desk she wouldn't get a chance to eat. There was always some crisis. At least this current crop of wedding guests seemed sensible; they were, in the main, a cheerful outdoorsy lot and today most of the party had headed into the mountains for a trek, some of the younger contingent taking kayaks onto the lake instead.

Unwrapping her sandwich, Maddie stretched her legs out, tilting her head to the sun. Bliss.

Only…she had the sense that someone was watching her. She gave the glade a quick glance around. Nothing. But Maddie couldn't shake off the feeling that she was definitely not alone. Had one of the castle dogs followed her out, looking for a bite of her sandwich? *'Ciao,'* she called out and waited, feeling a little foolish as she was answered with nothing but silence, until a branch rustled and a small, slim girl stepped into the clearing.

Maddie had had very little to do with children, and to her eyes the child could have been any age between five and ten. Her long, dark hair was in two messy braids, wisps escaping at every turn, and there were smears of dirt across her face, but Maddie noticed the cut of her torn shorts and the quality of her T-shirt. This urchin was expensively dressed—and didn't care about keeping her clothes neat.

'You look like you've been through the wars,' Maddie said in Italian.

The girl gave her a tentative smile. 'I've escaped.'

'Where from?'

'From the *castello*. My au pair wanted me to take a siesta. Sleep! On a day like this.' The girl looked scornfully up at the sky and Maddie had a moment's sneaking sympathy for the hapless au pair tasked with taming this wild child.

'It does seem a shame,' she agreed, breaking her sandwich in two and holding half out to the fugitive. 'Here, you must be hungry. I know adventuring always gave me an appetite when I was your age. I'm Maddie.'

'Arianna Falcone.'

Of course she was. Now Maddie could see the Conte in the proud tilt of the girl's chin, in the blue of her eyes. 'Nice to meet you, Arianna.'

'So this is where you're hiding?'

They both jumped guiltily as a stern voice echoed through the glade and Maddie felt her treacherous body jump to attention as the Conte strode into view. He looked cool despite the heat of the day, in well-cut linen trousers and a short-sleeved white shirt.

He took in the situation with one cool glance. 'Aiding and abetting my daughter, *signorina*?'

'Only with half a sandwich.' Maddie smiled at the unrepentant child.

'That's half a sandwich more than she deserves. *Piccola*, poor Isabella is looking everywhere for you. Go, find her and make your apologies.'

'But it's too lovely a day, Papa. I don't want a siesta.'

'Then, my child, you shouldn't have got caught. But, as you were, go and take your chastisement like a Falcone. Then, if you're good, we can go sailing this afternoon.'

The mutinous expression lightened and Arianna threw her arms around her father before taking off and running back in the direction of the castle, her half of Maddie's sandwich still clasped in her hand. To Maddie's surprise, and no little apprehension, the Conte made no move to follow his daughter, remaining in the glade and fixing Maddie with an inscrutable look. ·

With an inward sigh she put her own half-sandwich back in its bag. The cook had stuffed it full of mozzarella, rocket and sun-dried tomatoes; there was no way of eating it in any kind of dignified way, and Maddie needed all the dignity she could muster in front of this man.

'It's a lovely day.'

Small talk? Seriously. 'Yes.' Not the most articulate of responses, but all that expensive education teaching Maddie etiquette hadn't prepared her for how to answer when a man said one thing, but his body language said something quite different. Dante Falcone was ramrod-straight, gaze fixed firmly on her, looking more as if he was about to deliver a lecture rather than discuss the weather.

Deliver a lecture or devour her whole. Maddie curled her hands into fists, refusing to give in to the urge to smooth her red skirt down, but she couldn't help recalling what happened to girls in red who talked to wolf-eyed strangers in the woods.

Oh, what big eyes you have...

'Would you be kind enough to accompany me on a

short walk? There is something I would like to discuss with you.'

Maddie tried not to give her half-sandwich a longing look. She wanted to sit, eat and just be, not go for what was bound to be an excruciatingly uncomfortable walk. She had spent less than two hours in Dante Falcone's company and in those two hours he had deliberately embarrassed her, she had embarrassed herself, she'd been borderline rude several times. Why would she put herself through a second dose of that?

'Please,' he added. And then he smiled. And that changed everything.

The smile transformed Dante Falcone's face, softening the sharp, lean edges, transforming the saturnine look into something warmer, something Maddie wanted to get close to, his good looks no longer remote, statue-like, but flesh and blood and all the more attractive for that. Desire, new, hot and heavy, flooded through her, drying her throat and taking all capacity to think and reason away.

She reached for words, any words, but found none. Instead she nodded as he turned away towards a path she hadn't yet explored, supremely confident that she'd follow him. And she did, her feet powerless to disobey.

'You speak Italian very well.'

That was ironic; right now she could barely manage English. 'I went to a finishing school near Geneva. We spoke mostly French and Italian there.'

Maddie sensed rather than saw the rise of his elegant brows. 'And what brought you into event management?'

'I kind of fell into it,' she said carefully, but the Conte didn't react, merely waited for her to carry on and reluctantly she did. 'I grew up in a house a little like the Castello Falcone.'

'I see.'

There was no condemnation in the words, but Maddie couldn't help bristling. People often assumed that she'd spent her time floating around like some Jane Austen heroine, arranging flowers and making calls and considering it work. She straightened her shoulders, matching her pace with his. She was proud of what she had achieved. It would be nice if someone else was too.

'When I was growing up my family made a half-hearted effort to make Stilling Abbey pay its way; there was always a part of the roof to be repaired or a chronic case of damp or a huge heating bill. My parents thought allowing the public onto the premises once a month for two hours would be enough to raise some money—and they resented the mild intrusion of that. But when I was fifteen, I realised the reason why the much less architecturally and historically interesting manor house further along the valley was always busy—why they were actually making money—was that they made visitors feel welcome. That more opening hours, a café, a playground for the kids and space for weddings and parties were the key. All I had to do was convince my parents and find the money to get everything ready.'

It sounded so easy, summarised like that. But the reality was it had taken months to persuade her parents to open up the sacred ground of generations of Fitzroys to the general public five days a week, months to apply for the loans and grants to get the basic infrastructure in place. In return she had agreed to go abroad to finishing school for her A-level years. There might not have been money for the roof, but there was always money to ensure the children received the right kind of education. In Maddie's case an education which would enable her to marry well.

Her great-great-great-aunt might have been a famous suffragette, but feminism had yet to penetrate the thick medieval walls of Stilling Abbey.

'Impressive. Why did you leave?'

The old feelings of anger and unfairness hit her squarely in the chest and Maddie blew out a deep breath, almost welcoming the familiar bitterness as it washed away the last remnants of desire. 'The abbey is entailed along with the title.' Again she sensed Dante raising his eyebrows in surprise. 'And in England the title goes along to the eldest son, not the eldest child.'

'Same here, but titles are merely an historical anomaly and estates must be divided fairly amongst the children. My sister received half of my father's estate.'

'Not the *castello* though?' Maddie couldn't stop a sharp bitterness coating her voice.

'She lives in New Zealand so she had little use for it. But she also thought the Falcone ancestral home should stay with the title.'

'At least she had a choice.' Maddie speeded up her pace, furious with herself for giving so much away. She had loved every stone of the old abbey, known every inch of the grounds, thrown herself into making it a profitable concern—but it had been made very clear to her that she had no long-term future at her home. Her brother might care more for geology than history but the abbey was his. Maddie had even joined forces with other people in her position, eldest daughters, adopted children and children born outside of marriage, all disinherited by an old patriarchal system. But for all her justifiable anger she had been keenly aware just what a privileged problem being cut out of the succession to a title really was. In the end she had done her best to let go of the resentment and decided to do what she had been raised to do; marry into another ancient estate instead.

That hadn't turned out that well either.

Dante didn't say anything for a few long minutes and Maddie was relieved as she stomped along. That was all her past. No more aristocratic titles for her. The only time she would step inside a stately home would be in gainful employment or as a paying visitor—apart from the times she went back to Stilling Abbey as a visiting relative with a life of her own elsewhere.

No. She had a plan. Over the next few years she intended to find out who she was when she wasn't an Honourable, wasn't the daughter, sister or wife of someone deemed more worthy because of his Y chromosome.

See what she was worth apart from her value as a blue-blooded brood mare. If anyone would ever look at her the way her ex-fiancé looked at his soon-to-be wife.

'Is that why you came here? For a fresh start?'

Maddie sucked in a breath, surprised at the insight in the casual question. 'Partly. I wanted to get away from the UK, to travel, to stand on my own two feet—but that takes money and I don't have any of my own.' She glanced at him with a self-mocking smile. 'One doesn't need anything as common as wages when one lives at home and waits for a suitable Duke or Earl to come along. I'm here for the cold, hard cash.' And to get away from England and her old life, but there was no need for Dante to know about that. She'd exposed enough already.

'And then?'

'Travelling,' she said promptly. 'I am going to see the world.'

'All of it?'

'As much as I can. I'm going to work my way around. One thing every girl who has grown up in a huge, falling-apart house knows how to do is use their hands. I can waitress, clean, muck out horses, pick fruit. I'm not afraid to get my hands dirty.'

'What *are* you afraid of?' His voice was soft, reflective, almost as if he was asking himself the question.

How could she answer that when the choice was so wide? Afraid she would never have a perfect kiss? That no one would ever look at her as if she was the most desirable being in the world? That she would never know who she really was? She'd never admit that to the tall, dark man next to her.

'I'm a Fitzroy. We don't admit to fear.'

Their walk had taken them deeper into the pine forests which populated the mountain shelf on which San Tomo and the lake resided, the path beginning to wind up into the slopes. Dante stopped and turned and Maddie followed suit, surprised to see they had already begun to make their way uphill along the meandering path. The valley spread out before them, the lake reflecting the brilliant blue of the sky. In the centre of their eye line the graceful spires of the Castello Falcone soared, mirroring the mountains behind.

'My sister is coming to stay next week,' Dante said abruptly and Maddie glanced at him, sensing that the reason for this unexpected walk might become clear.

'That's nice.' Sometimes banalities were the best thing to fall back on. That she *had* learned at finishing school; Small Talk for Beginners.

His mouth quirked into a half-smile and Maddie's heart gave a skip. '*Sì*. We are close, Luciana and I. She...' He paused. 'She worries about me. About Arianna.'

'Oh?' Maddie's mind raced. She knew little about her employer, but she had heard that he was a widower, that his young, beautiful actress wife had died tragically in a car crash on the sometimes treacherous road down to Milan. There was some kind of mystery, a hint of scandal, but she had never enquired further. She knew all too well how easily rumours could start, how things could be misrepresented.

'She thinks I need a partner, that Arianna needs a mother. She has many friends who she considers suitable.'

'She would get on very well with my mother. She is always sending me details of potential husbands.' It had taken less than a month since Maddie had walked away from the altar unwed for her mother to suggest a new groom.

'Luciana is under the impression that I am in a relationship. A romantic relationship,' he clarified, his brows drawing across his forehead as he spoke.

'Under the impression?' Maddie couldn't stop the grin spreading across her face. 'How did that happen?'

Dante drew himself up, the very epitome of dignity— if it wasn't for the guilty expression in his eyes, rather like that of a small boy caught out in mischief. 'I may have told her a small falsehood,' he admitted and Maddie's grin widened. 'For the best of reasons. It made her happy to think I was dating and it stopped her trying to set me up with her friends. It seemed like a good idea at the time to invent a short-term relationship that would end amicably in a few months' time.'

Why on earth was he telling her this? 'But now she's coming to visit? That's awkward. Could you pretend that your mystery girlfriend has had to go away on business? Or maybe she just dumped you?'

'She dumped me?' Dante couldn't have sounded more outraged if they had been discussing a real relationship.

'Of course, otherwise there's no reason for your sister not to keep setting you up. Pretend you're nursing a broken heart and you need some time to regroup.' Judging by the confusion in Dante's eyes he didn't often get teased. It was nice to turn the tables on him.

'The problem is...' He took a deep breath and apprehension curled Maddie's stomach as he turned to her, pride, embarrassment and an indefinable heat that Maddie could feel in every nerve ending in his gaze. 'The problem is, she's under the impression that I am in a relationship with you. So, Maddie Fitzroy. I was hoping that you might do me a favour and pretend to be my girlfriend for the next few weeks. A young lady with your birth and education should be able to carry it off perfectly. What do you say?'

Her birth? Her education? Not Maddie herself, but her genes. Again. Would she ever get to be just Maddie? She tilted her head, every inch the Honourable once again. 'I'm sorry, *signor*, but I am afraid what you're asking is impossible.'

'Why?'

'Why? You must see that it's out of the question!'

'Not at all. I've told her that the relationship is in its early stages, so she won't be expecting an established couple. She's only spending a week here before going to see our mother in Lucerne. We will say that you're very busy with your work. That way you have a perfect excuse not to spend too much time with us—and when it's unavoidable I'm sure you will manage admirably. You have the necessary qualities to cope.'

The necessary qualities? No matter where she ran, was she always going to be seen as nothing more than a convenient consort? No, worse; here she was nothing more than an *imaginary* convenient consort.

'How kind of you to say so,' she said, every word bitten off as coldly as she could manage. 'But I'm afraid I must still decline your offer. I have to get back to work now. It's been...' She paused, searching for the right word. 'It's been interesting talking to you. Goodbye.'

As Maddie turned and stalked away, she was conscious of another emotion trying to dig its way through her indignation. Disappointment.

The Conte discombobulated her; she wasn't sure she liked him at all. But she was drawn to him on some primal level, in a way she had never experienced before. Maddie hadn't known what to expect from their walk, but a small part of her had thrilled to the heat she had sensed between them, had wanted to discover more.

But it looked as if she had imagined the heat. That the only attraction she had for the Conte was through her name and her convenient background. It was an all too familiar story. But this time she was saying no.

CHAPTER FOUR

HE HAD ONE day to come up with a plan—and so far he had nothing.

Dante swivelled and looked at his great-great-grandfather's portrait for inspiration. None was forthcoming. Maybe it was for the best. Maybe it was time for Dante to have a long overdue discussion with his sister. To tell her the truth.

His chest tightened. It wasn't just that he didn't want to upset her, for her to know he had deceived her. It wasn't even that it was easier to bury every feeling apart from his love and protectiveness for Arianna, rather than face the mess he had made of his life and marriage. It was knowing how vulnerable confiding the truth to his sister would make him.

She knew some of it. Knew Violetta had been unhappy. Knew she had cheated on him. Knew he blamed himself for throwing his energies into work rather than repairing his tattered marriage. But she didn't know how he had been duped. Didn't know that Violetta had never loved him. Didn't know that he had loved a phantom.

A marriage gone wrong was a tragedy. A marriage based on deceit was nothing but a sick joke and he the fool at the centre. Five years later it still haunted him, the knowledge of how easily—how willingly—he had been duped.

He stilled as he heard footsteps approaching the door. Nobody visited the old picture gallery; it wasn't part of the publicly accessible part of the castle. That was why he came here to think—he could always count on being alone.

The handle turned, the door opened—and Maddie stood in the entrance, her face mirroring the shock he was sure was on his, before she concealed it with a polite smile.

Dante was getting very used to that particularly polite expression. It wasn't blank, more a carefully smooth look, the kind which could take the user from a hospital visit to a diplomatic lunch without causing offence to anyone. It served her well; he'd seen it employed to calm a drunkenly belligerent wedding guest, to soothe a chef when she'd informed him of three unexpected food intolerances which threatened to destroy a planned menu.

And she used it with him, every time they inadvertently met. It was different from the open, sunny smile she greeted her co-workers with, different from the affectionate, almost conspiratorial grin she shared with Arianna, who seemed to have latched on to her.

'I'm sorry,' Maddie said, every bit the professional. Her dress was spotless and cool-looking despite the advancing hour and the heat of the day, not a hair in her neat chignon out of place, her make-up discreet and fresh. 'I didn't realise anyone would be in here. I'll come back later...'

She took a step backwards, her hand on the door. It would be easier to let her walk away, to continue to brood alone, but Dante halted her. 'Don't leave on my account. What do you need in here?'

'Oh, well, one of my brides wants to dress in a historically accurate way, but doesn't know where to start. I offered to send her some pictures of the past Contessas to give her inspiration. I did warn her that there are a lot of different styles, but she doesn't know if she wants renaissance or reunification so I'll need to photo a selection.' She raised the small camera she held as if proving her words.

'Come in. Take your photographs.'

After a quick glance at him, Maddie stepped warily into the room. 'Thank you. I won't be long.'

Dante nodded and resumed his study of his great-great-grandfather but all his concentration had disappeared; instead he was keenly aware of every step Maddie took. Aware of the way she sized up the pictures, the focus on her face as she photographed the suitable ones, the swiftly hidden amusement at some of the more outlandish dresses. And he knew the exact moment she stopped in front of the portrait of Violetta he had commissioned for their wedding.

'She was beautiful, yes?' he said, not looking at either Maddie or the portrait.

'Very.' She paused. 'I'm sorry I couldn't help with your sister. Have you come up with a solution?'

'Not yet.' Dante took a deep breath as he turned and looked at Maddie—and at the portrait. The two women couldn't have been more different, Violetta dark, her lush curves poured into a designer ball gown, her eyes proud, smile mocking, a stark contrast to Maddie's blonde slenderness and neat, efficient look. 'I'm sure I'll think of something.'

'Of course. I'm sure you will.' Maddie turned away, heading back to the door before stopping and swivelling to look back at him. 'It's just... I can't help wondering why you lied to her in the first place. I get that you're close, that you don't want her to worry, but why does she care so much? I want my brother to be happy, of course I do, but I wouldn't fuss him to the stage where he started propositioning random employees to lie to me and pretend they were in a relationship.'

Put like that, the whole scheme did sound a little insane—if you didn't know Luciana, that was.

'I'm sorry,' Maddie said quickly. 'As I said, really it's none of my business.'

But it was. Dante had made it her business when he had tried to involve her. And no matter what he told Luciana tomorrow, when she arrived at the *castello* and met Maddie her curiosity would be piqued. The name and description were a perfect match after all. Luciana would be bound to wonder why Dante had chosen this particular woman as the model for his pretend girlfriend, would be bound to come up with all kinds of crazy theories.

And they would be crazy. Wouldn't they?

Dante looked over at Maddie, cool and poised, her calm gaze fixed on him as she waited for an answer. Maddie was very attractive, of course. They had only just met. That was why she had been the first person to come to mind; there was no more to his choice than that.

He could see Luciana's mocking look as she took apart that explanation all too clearly. He was going to have to come up with a better reason than that.

'My sister introduced me to Violetta.' Dante saw the moment Maddie's glance flew to the portrait, watched her eyes soften, and he winced.

'I see.'

But of course she didn't. She probably believed, as so many others did, that his heart had died with his wife. That the reason he hadn't dated again, was still single five years later, was that no one could replace the beautiful young Contessa.

For some reason he didn't want Maddie to believe that. The truth might be uglier but it was real. 'I was only twenty-two.' It was like talking about someone else; Dante didn't even remember that carefree boy with the world at his feet. 'My father had recently died and I had inherited the title and half the family business. It was a lot to take on—and Luciana was about to move to New Zealand with her husband to help run his winery. My mother had already left for Switzerland and so all the family fortune was in my inexperienced hands. Luciana was worried about leaving me, insisted on spending all the time she had left in Italy with me—and that's when I met Violetta.'

He stepped closer to the portrait and gazed up at his wife, memories flooding him as he tried to sort out the truth from the fictions—the fictions she had woven, fictions he'd willingly believed. 'She was several years older than me—our paths would probably never have crossed if it weren't for Luciana. But when they did...' He closed his eyes briefly. 'Violetta got pregnant very quickly. It wasn't planned, but of course I offered to marry her.' It wasn't just an offer; he'd jumped at the opportunity. It wasn't until much later that he'd begun to wonder just how much of an accident the pregnancy had been.

'We didn't know each other very well, not in all the ways a husband and wife should know each other before they make their vows. The truth is it wasn't a very successful marriage.' Dante winced at the understatement of the century. 'Apart from Arianna, of course. I can't—I *don't*—regret anything that resulted in my daughter; Luciana knows this. She feels responsible and nothing I say changes that.'

Maddie took another step forward, until she was almost close enough to touch, close enough so that Dante could see the concern in her grey eyes. 'But I still don't understand why you need to pretend to be in a relationship—with me or anyone. I mean, you're tall, dark and not too horrendous to look at. You seem to have all your own teeth—and what have I forgotten? Oh, yes, you're rich, titled and own a castle; you're a great dad. Surely nice, compatible women must be queuing up around the block. If you're not still in love with your wife then what is stopping you from dating any of those women? You'd get your sister off your back and have some fun while you're at it. Why go to all this subterfuge?'

'I drove my wife away. That's why she died. Arianna is without a mother because of me and she has to come first. I have no time and no inclination to pursue any kind of relationship.' Dante snapped his mouth closed. He'd said too much. He swallowed, moderating his tone with some effort. 'My sister has been unwell. I didn't want her upsetting herself further about me or Arianna. But it was wrong of me to lie, wrong of me to drag you into it. Please accept my apologies.'

Maddie looked up at the portrait again. Violetta Falcone had been a stunning woman, all fire and passion and pride. No wonder the Conte had fallen so hard for her. And how could she fault him for lying to make his sister happy? Maddie understood all about family pressure; after all, she had spent so much of her life trying to make her parents happy, to get their approval.

She'd finally realised that nothing that fulfilled her would satisfy them, that they couldn't see past their own small, narrow world and wanted her contained within it. Dante's lies came from love. How could she fault him for that? All she had ever wanted was unconditional love. It had taken almost marrying a man who *didn't* love her for her to realise that.

Dante wasn't asking for a lifetime. He wanted a mere week.

And would a week with him be such a terrible thing?

She slid a glance his way. His lips were pressed together, expression shuttered, as if he hadn't just confided in her in a way she suspected the proud Conte seldom confided in anyone. Her stomach tumbled as she took him in. The expanse of olive skin exposed at his throat, the sharp cheekbones, the sensuous curve of his mouth. Maddie swallowed, desire pulsing through her. No. Spending more time with Dante Falcone wouldn't be that terrible at all.

She had told herself that she would never be anyone's convenient relationship again. But the Conte needed her. Maybe not physically or emotionally, but he still needed her. And she needed to step out of her hiding place sooner rather than later. Out of her comfort zone. To confront her fears—and her desire.

Maddie took a deep breath. 'A plane ticket.' To her surprise her voice was strong, even though she quivered at the thought of the deal she was about to propose.

Dante's brows shot up.

'And overtime. Double time for any time I spend with you and your sister. But no one here must know what we are doing. I don't want any gossip or speculation and it wouldn't be fair for your daughter to think we were dating. So you need to tell your sister that we are keeping things quiet for now because we are seeing where things are going. Those are my terms.' Maddie's heart hammered as she spoke. What on earth was she doing? Could she really handle a week in Dante Falcone's company?

'Why have you changed your mind?' His glance was sharp, penetrating, as if he could see straight through her, to that pathetic need to be wanted, to be needed.

Maddie straightened her shoulders. This was different. He *did* need her—which meant she held all the cards. 'Because I realised that this could be a mutually beneficial deal. And because, although I don't think you should have lied to your sister, I understand why you did. Your motives were good.'

'She arrives tomorrow.'

'Then we'd better get our stories straight—if my terms are acceptable.'

'Very acceptable.' He held out his hand and, after an infinitesimal pause, Maddie took it. His fingers closed around hers, strong and sure, his touch scalding through her body.

Did she really believe she held all the cards? Suddenly she wasn't so sure. 'Good. That's decided.' She stepped back, her hand cold, empty as she loosened it from his. 'What next?'

'Next we need to get our stories straight, to decide on how we met, what we were wearing, what we spoke about—believe me, we must have every detail agreed; there is nothing so small my sister won't want to know.'

The enormity of what she had agreed to shivered through her. This wasn't just about having a few friendly chats with Dante's sister. This was about pretending to be falling in love. Something she knew nothing about. 'Then we had better schedule a meeting.' The business-like term was reassuring. She could do business.

'A meeting sounds delightful.' Maddie's eyes narrowed at the amusement in the Conte's voice. 'But maybe a little formal in light of the situation? Let me take you out for dinner somewhere away from here and we can talk properly there. Where do you prefer? Riva? Milan? We could even make it to Verona for the evening if we leave soon. Or do you prefer the mountain restaurants? The trattoria in the next valley is very good, but we are more likely to be recognised there. We could go a few valleys over; have you been to the Russo Leone? It used to be very good and it's a little more discreet.'

'I haven't been to any of those places. I actually haven't left San Tomo yet...' Maddie's voice trailed off as Dante fixed her with an incredulous expression.

'Scuzi?'

'The food at the *castello* is so good, I usually eat here, or cook for myself. Occasionally I go out to the *ristorante* in the village. I just haven't had a chance to explore further afield.'

'But you've been here for, what, nine months?'

'Ten.'

'But what do you do on your days off?'

She cringed a little inside at the shock in his voice. 'I don't really have days off.'

Dante stared at Maddie, but she couldn't meet his eyes. 'We overwork you so much?'

'No, no, I just like to make sure everything is okay. I may have a slight tendency to control-freakery.'

'A *slight* tendency?'

She scowled. 'Okay. I am a complete control freak, but that's what these brides need. Someone here all the time so every niggle is smoothed out straight away. They expect me to be on call twenty-four hours a day while they are here...'

'And on the two days in between?'

'The next bride usually needs a lot of reassurance in the forty-eight hours leading up to her wedding,' she said defensively. 'I'm not in the office *all* the time. I go for walks. Read a book...'

'Madeleine, why are you here?'

'I told you. To save up, to get away...'

'You came to Italy for that, but surely you could have saved more and quicker if you'd stayed at home.'

Of course she could have. Dante paid her well—but she had elected not to live in the castle and even with her frugal, hard-working lifestyle that made it harder to save enough to start her travels. The overtime and plane ticket she had agreed with Dante would be a welcome addition to her savings. Maddie lifted her chin and finally met his keen gaze. 'I needed to get away, to be somewhere new, to be someone different.'

His expression was all too understanding. 'You want to be somewhere different. You want to start your adventures and yet, *signorina*, you hide behind your work, not exploring anything this place has to offer. I wonder if it's the lack of a plane ticket holding you back from starting a new life, or whether it's you?' He inclined his head in a brief gesture of farewell. 'I'll pick you up in three hours. Dress smartly.'

Maddie didn't say a word as Dante smoothly negotiated the car around the mountain curves; she was still hearing the echoes of his earlier parting shot.

How *dared* he accuse her of holding back? He knew nothing about her.

But the truth of his words stung. She *was* scared. Scared that if she stripped away the purpose that had always fuelled her then there would be nothing left. That no one would notice her at all.

So maybe she should treat this week like an opportunity. At the end of it she would have her plane ticket and enough saved up to start her new life. Let this next week be a practice for her new life. Forget the old, dignified, playing by the rules Maddie and become the kind of person who saw every turn in the road as an opportunity.

Starting with the man sitting next to her, lean hands carelessly on the wheel, the flex in his muscles effortless as he manoeuvred the car through hairpin bends. Because, painfully insightful as he may have been about her, he had also revealed an equal amount about himself.

So his marriage had been no fairy tale? At least he had tried, had staked everything on love. The gamble might have failed, but as someone who had been about to walk, eyes wide open, into a marriage based on trust, friendship and convenience, how could Maddie blame anyone else for wanting more from their life? Better to risk it all and lose than never to risk at all.

But when Dante Falcone lost he just walked away, closing himself off from love and hope like some mythical beast, hiding behind his castle walls. So afraid that his sister or that anyone would see his vulnerabilities that he preferred to pay for a temporary girlfriend than admit his fallibility.

But Maddie had seen a crack in his walls that day by the lake. Not just in the way he had responded, the way he had looked at her, but in the way he had needled her, provoked her afterwards.

She had got under his skin.

A smile curved her mouth. *She had got under his skin*. Of course she had. Why else would he have used her face, her name, for his imaginary girlfriend?

And, she admitted, he had got under hers. Otherwise why would she have agreed to this insanity? The plane ticket and overtime would ensure she could leave at the end of the summer, sure. But was it really the money—or was it the game that had tempted her?

She'd never had the opportunity to play before.

Here was her chance and she had nothing to lose.

Lost in her thoughts, Maddie barely noticed her surroundings until Dante manoeuvred the car around the last hairpin bend and the glory of Lake Garda was spread out below: impossibly blue, ringed with mountains, ancient villages perched high above or clinging to the water's edge. Maddie was incredibly fond of their own lake, but, biased as she was, she had to admit that San Tomo paled into insignificance beside this awe-inspiring expanse of water. She sat forward, eagerly taking in every detail as they drove the last few miles towards the lake and the buzzing town of Riva, with its cobbled streets and cosmopolitan air. Why had she kept herself hidden away in her valley like some kind of lesser-tressed Rapunzel when all this was on her doorstep?

To Maddie's surprise, Dante bypassed the road to Riva, sweeping past the turn-off, heading instead towards a small harbour right at the very head of the lake. He pulled into a small car park and, before Maddie had a chance to even gather her thoughts, her car door was opened for her and a young man in a smart white nauti-

cal uniform inclined his head as he helped her step out
of the low-slung sports car.

She looked around, glad to be standing on her own
two feet, her stomach a little uneasy after the fast, curving drive despite Dante's expert handling of the vehi-
cle. They were standing in a small glade. A short path
cut through the trees leading to a wooden jetty where a
beautiful small yacht was moored. Another young man
in the same white uniform stood on the deck, busily coil-
ing ropes in a way that looked competently nautical to
her inexperienced eyes. She looked questioningly up at
Dante as he joined her.

'I didn't want our conversation to be overheard,' he
said by way of curt explanation, and then he smiled, that
same sudden smile which had so comprehensively dis-
armed her before. 'Besides, you said you hadn't explored
the area. What better way to see the lake than to be *on*
the lake? We have several hours before it gets dark yet.
The sunset is incredible viewed from the water.'

There was nothing she could say to this apart from
'thank you' and within ten minutes Maddie found herself seated on a comfortable padded bench on one side
of a table set for two as the yacht cast off, edging out
onto the still evening lake. Small flotillas were making
their way into shore, pleasure cruisers processing in a
stately fashion up and down the lake and other yachts
and boats could be seen dotting the lake as far as Maddie could see.

'This is lovely,' she said, accepting a Bellini with a
smile at the waiter and took the handwritten menu he
was proffering her. And it was. Even with the artificial-
ity and awkwardness of the situation, some of the cares
Maddie carried with her twenty-four hours a day seemed

suddenly not to be quite so important. So the Hathaway dress hadn't arrived yet? So the chef was threatening to take his leave during the Johnson nuptials, offended by the amount of dietary requirements emailed in? So the Lastinghams needed four-hour extra staff to ensure the bride's warring parents were never left alone at any time during their five-day stay? It would work out. It always did. And after all, they were only weddings—it was the marriage that counted and only the couple at the heart of all the frivolity and flounce had any sway over that.

For the first few moments they talked sparingly, comments confined to their menu choices, the beauty of the landscape and the elegance of the yacht, but once they had both ordered and the waiters had refilled their glasses and set olives and tiny bruschetta topped with fresh tomato, peppers and anchovies in front of them, Maddie knew it was time to step up a gear or two.

'Okay,' she said after she'd popped a bruschetta into her mouth, almost swooning at the perfect balance of garlic, salt, olive and tangy tomato. 'Let's do this.'

Dante leaned back in his seat, one hand curved elegantly around his glass, eyes gleaming with amusement—and an interest that Maddie could feel zapping right through her body all the way down to her toes. '*Bene*. Why don't you start? Tell me about yourself.'

Maddie took a long sip of her drink before setting her glass down and regarding Dante. 'A one-woman monologue on the origins of Madeleine Fitzroy? That doesn't sound like much fun for either of us. Let's make this a little more interesting. How about we play twenty questions? I ask you five questions, anything I want. And you can ask me five in turn. But we have to be prepared to answer our own questions...'

'Any questions?' The gleam in his eyes had intensified and Maddie reached for her glass, needing the support of a task, any task, to give her a reason to break eye contact, which seemed suddenly more intense than she could handle.

'As long as you're prepared to answer the same question honestly,' she said as coolly as possible.

For an impossibly long moment the Conte simply looked at her, his blue eyes unreadable, and then, just as the tension had risen to an almost unbearable pitch, he nodded. '*Si.* I agree. So, my first question. Have you ever been in love?'

CHAPTER FIVE

MADDIE STARED. HAD she *what*?

First off, this was an unfair question because hadn't Dante Falcone already told her that he'd been besotted with his wife, so he was one up on her already? Secondly, she'd expected that they would start off with where they were born and favourite colours—innocuous warm-up questions; not go straight in for the million-dollar round.

And, thirdly, she wasn't sure of the answer.

'I...' She stopped and took another sip of the Bellini, her mind racing. She was twenty-six years old; she had been engaged to be married. But had she ever been in love? Infatuated? Besotted?

But she knew she was prevaricating. There was only one honest answer.

Maddie put the drink down and looked over at Dante. 'No. I've never been in love. The nearest I came was a crush on my ski instructor when I was at finishing school—but we all had crushes on our ski instructors; it was a rite of passage. Actually Daisy Anstruther-Jones married hers. It was a fearful scandal, but they're still married, she had twins last year and they run a ski school just outside Geneva, so really it all worked out for the best for her.'

She tried not to sigh. Lucky Daisy. Maddie had envied her even then, despite the gossip and thinking eighteen was very young for such a commitment. Daisy hadn't cared that Matt didn't have a trust fund or a title or connections— she had ignored all her family's pleas and threats and followed her heart. If only Maddie's heart had ever felt so sure about anything or anyone.

'And did your ski instructor return your feelings?'

Maddie raised her eyebrows. 'Is that one of your questions? Either way I don't reply to another question until you answer yours. Have *you* ever been in love?'

She thought she knew the answer, but Dante didn't reply and the silence went on and on until he said just one, bleak word. 'No.'

'Oh.'

'I thought I was. But the woman I loved didn't exist. I had no idea who Violetta was, not truly. I fell for a face and a façade. So, no. Never. And yet...' He took a sip of his drink. 'It felt real. A reminder that romantic love can't be trusted. I won't make that mistake again.'

Maddie was beginning to regret her impulsive suggestion of a game; it was all getting too dark far too soon. Too real. With a relief she looked up and saw the waiter approaching, their first courses on a gleaming silver tray, and she waited until her *risotto al funghi* had been placed before her before speaking.

'I'm sorry. I know what's it like to be engaged to someone you're not in love with—but I can't imagine how much more difficult it is to be married and in the same situation. It must have been very lonely.'

Dante's eyes met hers, surprise and relief mingling in their depths. 'That's exactly what it was. Very lonely—

loneliness compounded with the knowledge that I was a fool.'

'You were twenty-two, weren't you? If you can't make mistakes in your early twenties, when can you? And at least you have the excuse of *thinking* you were in love. You were brave enough to make the leap. That has to count for something.'

'And you? How did you manage to get engaged without love? And yes, this is my second question.'

Maddie picked up a fork and prodded her risotto, the rich aroma a little less enticing than it had been a few moments ago. 'If I was ever in love with anything it wasn't a person—it was a place. My home. It's like nowhere else, hidden in the middle of the rolling Downs, surrounded by forests and gardens and fields—most of the abbey was torn down by Henry VIII, but the old refectory is part of the house and the ruins can be seen all about the gardens. I spent my childhood playing on them the way other children play on swings and climbing frames. But, as I told you, my brother is to inherit even though he was never interested in running a big estate, and when I turned twenty-three my mother made it clear that I needed to find a home of my own, even after I'd turned the estate around, started to make a profit for the first time in decades.'

She fell silent as she scooped up a portion of the risotto, the rich, aromatic flavours going a little way to unravel the knot in her stomach. 'Anyway, to cut a long, dull story short, I went to stay with my godparents— my godfather had just been diagnosed with severe heart problems and his wife was finding it hard to cope—and so I just took over there. Flintock Hall is set on a large estate just like the abbey and even though they didn't open to the public there were still tenants and staff and estate managers to deal with. And I did. It meant Lady Navenby could concentrate on her husband and their son, Theo, could stay in London and work. He came back at weekends though and we spent a lot of time together.' Her voice trailed off and she summoned up her best social smile as she glanced over at the silent Dante.

'I'm not sure who thought of marriage first, although I know Theo's mother was very keen on the match. And as Lord Navenby's health weakened he began to worry about the succession. He wanted to know Theo was safe and happy before he died, that there would be an heir to the Earldom, that his name would continue. Somehow it just became common knowledge, became assumed that I would marry Theo, provide the heir, and in return I would get the home I needed. That's how it's done, right? We trade our fortunes, our lineage for a title and a home. Tale older than time. Then, one night, when Lord Navenby was in hospital and fading fast, we were told he only had days, not weeks. We were in shock. He'd seemed to rally a little, so we weren't expecting... Anyway, emotions were running high and when Theo drove me back to the hall he kissed me for the first time. For comfort, I think. If there were no fireworks, well, it wasn't horrid either. And then he asked me to marry him. I wasn't coerced into it. It made so much sense; the fact we didn't love each other seemed irrelevant. We liked each other well enough.'

'So what happened?'

'We got right to the wedding day. I was in a white dress, the marquees were set up, guests had arrived— we got all the way to the altar. And it hit me. Just what I was doing. That my whole life would be one long, even plane. No passion. No huge unhappiness either, possibly, but no huge joy. Every day the same. That I was selling myself short. I just couldn't do it. No house, no security was worth a lifetime of polite existence with someone who merely liked me. I'd spent my childhood living like that. I knew I wanted more. And,' she added, forking up another scoop of risotto, 'it turned out he was in love with someone else anyway; he was just too much of a gentleman to jilt me so close to the wedding.'

'You got all the way to the altar and called it off?' Dante's expression was full of admiration and it warmed Maddie through to see it. She was so used to being an object of pity or amusement. No one had ever admired her impulsive action before. 'That took some courage.'

The hard shell with which Maddie had encased herself ever since her wedding cracked a little and she blinked back sudden, hot tears. 'I just couldn't say vows I didn't mean, pledge myself to a man who wanted *what* I was, not who I was. Even though I think it was the only time my mother had ever really been proud of me...' She stopped, embarrassed at having revealed so much. 'Anyway. There was quite a lot of publicity—Theo is an Earl and successful in his own right, and my dad is a Baron; the family has links going back to the Norman Conquest. It doesn't mean anything, not really, but the gossip papers and blogs loved the whole blue-blooded nonsense. They called me the Runaway Bride and followed me everywhere until I came here.'

'So *that's* why you came here? Why you've barely left the valley?'

'I know it seems silly. I wasn't that famous. The publicity was more of an inconvenience, an embarrassment, than anything really serious. But I liked the anonymity I found here. Liked being out of sight and out of mind. The only thing is, Theo is getting married in a few weeks—and this wedding will definitely go ahead. It might stir things up again. That's why I want to get on with the next stage in my plans and leave Europe altogether sooner rather than later. Just disappear for a while.'

Maddie waited until the waiter had taken away her risotto, replacing it with the chicken she had ordered, served with fresh sautéed vegetables and a delicious-looking sauce before she spoke again, glad of the opportunity to turn the conversation to lighter topics. 'My question, I think. If you could have any superpower, what would it be and why?'

Dante blinked, his fork, half-filled with his own meal, arrested halfway to his mouth. 'My what?'

'Superpower. That's my first question.'

'To read minds. To know what people are really thinking beyond the words and the smiles.' His own smile was grim and Maddie knew he was thinking of Violetta. So much for lighter conversation.

'I don't think I would want to know what's in people's heads. Too much information in every way. I would want to fly. Then I wouldn't need to wait for a plane ticket, I could just take off and land anywhere.'

'The flyaway bride, not the runaway bride?'

The joke was so unexpected that Maddie could only stare in disbelief before breaking into a grin as she imagined the scenario. 'My veil billowing out behind me? My mother would have been even more furious than she already was—that veil was antique lace! Okay, another one. What animal would you be if you could turn into any animal at all?'

Dante leaned back, his eyes narrowed in amusement,

that smile back on his face. Maddie tried not to let her gaze linger on his mouth, glad that he couldn't actually read her mind as she followed every curve of his lips, the finely sculpted lines of his austerely handsome face. 'A falcon, *naturalmente.* According to family legend, my ancestor could indeed turn into a bird of prey, to spy on his enemies.'

'Handy party trick.'

'And you?'

'Right now a sloth sounds pretty appealing. I've never known how to just stop and relax; maybe it would be good to have some enforced downtime in the sun.'

'Interesting choice. Are sloths on your list of things to see?'

'Pretty much at the top,' Maddie admitted. 'I'm planning to go west, not east, head to the US, work my way right through Central America—via the sloths—into South America.'

'Intrepid.'

'I haven't done it yet.' There was a world's difference in planning and doing. Maddie knew that all too well. There were so many things she had never done: slept in a tent or a hostel—although she had survived boarding school—carried her belongings on her back, cooked over a campfire, worked in a bar, travelled by bus. She could plan to her heart's content, download itineraries and timetables, but taking that first step—that had still to be proven. She still had to summon up the courage to put a lifetime of wanting to be needed, to be occupied, of proving herself through service behind her and just live for the moment.

Maddie eyed the man opposite. She doubted Dante Falcone ever allowed himself to live for the moment either. Never allowed himself a single impulsive decision since the day he had fallen for a woman he never really knew at all. Not until he lied to his sister and pretended that he was in a relationship with Maddie herself. She had to learn to be free—it was a lesson he could do with as well.

Over the rest of the excellent dinner Dante found out that Maddie's favourite colour was cobalt-blue and, after some thought, decided his was the exact shade of brown of his daughter's eyes. He admitted a teenage dream to become an artist, while Maddie explained she had agreed to attend the Swiss finishing school because her parents allowed her to sign up for an online business and marketing course at the same time. 'Girls like me have two choices,' she'd said as they waited for their tiramisu to be served. 'The brainy ones go to Oxford and Cambridge or somewhere with a decent helping of People Like Us: Bristol, Edinburgh, St Andrew's, of course, and make connections to help them in their high-powered careers, whilst the really forward-thinking ones bag a husband at the same time. The less brainy go to finishing schools and learn to make a decent *cordon bleu* meal and put on a dinner party; or they take a secretarial course and get a PA job in the City *or* look superior in a Chelsea art gallery until *they* bag a husband. It's all still very 1950s. My parents had no idea what to do with a daughter who just wanted to learn about return on investment and profit margins, so we compromised. Not for the first time.'

Over the excellent tiramisu they had each chosen their desert island books—the *Aeneid* for Dante, *Pride and Prejudice* for Maddie—and their desert island music. His a live recording of *La Bohème* from La Scala and

Maddie, after much agonising, had decided, to his equal agony, on her own personal Taylor Swift playlist.

'So,' Maddie said when they had established their favourite places and chosen their final meals, 'I call that a success—I think we know a reasonable amount about each other now. Enough for people who have only known each other for a few weeks anyway.'

Dante couldn't help but agree. Disconcerting as Maddie's game had been at the beginning, it had actually been fun to try and decide whether he would want a classic steak or a really good plate of pasta for a last meal and to listen to why Maddie thought Costa Rica was her perfect place, even though she hadn't been there yet. In fact he didn't remember being as relaxed or entertained since...well, since his father had died, his sister had moved away and he had assumed the mantle of the Falcone empire.

Even when it was just he and Arianna together he found it hard to relax. He had to be father and mother both, confidant and tutor, indulgent parent and strict teacher. Good cop and bad cop. And this was the easy stage—her teen years were getting ever closer, with all the worry they were bound to bring.

'Agreed. I still don't know how any civilised person could want baked beans for their last meal...'

'On white buttered toast!'

'Nor do I see the attraction of a creature that sleeps the whole time, but I will try and read *Pride and Prejudice*. Or,' he amended, 'I will watch the film.'

'No, the television series. You need to be completely absorbed in it.'

'Maybe,' he said cautiously, not wanting to commit himself to too many hours watching English people drink tea and dance at balls. 'Shall we take our coffees and go and sit at the prow of the boat? The sun will set soon and the view should be quite spectacular.'

Maddie nodded assent and got up from the table. Dante took a minute to admire her long, coltish legs, displayed to advantage in the short full skirt of her silver dress, her arms bared by the thin straps, hair loose and flowing down her back. She was, he had to admit, looking magnificent, all tanned limbs and tousled hair. He followed her to the front of the yacht and stood beside her as she leaned on the ship rail, looking out over the water to the mountains and the reddening sun. The deckhands had cleared their plates and melted silently away, the captain out of sight in the cabin above. It was as if they were all alone on the wide lake under the pink-streaked sky and suddenly, despite the freshness of the evening air all around them, Dante's lungs constricted, his chest tightening. It was a setting made for romance—but he was done with romance. This evening was all about business and all the jokes and dreams they'd shared didn't change that.

'How long does your sister think we've been dating?'

There, Maddie felt it too. That need to keep the conversation businesslike in such seductive surroundings.

'Less than a month. We are at a very early stage in our relationship. I haven't been to the *castello* since last summer, Luciana knows that, but there is no reason we couldn't have met for meetings in Milan.'

'Hmm.' She wrinkled her nose as she turned to him, and Dante couldn't look away from its perfect pertness. 'I've already told you I have never been in love. Before Theo I dated several very nice, very acceptable men but quite frankly would much rather have been planning a new pathway through the wood or organising an event than spend too much time exchanging sweet nothings with them. And they felt the same—I was more of a useful trophy, someone to stand at the side of a rugby match and cheer or a decorative escort to social events they couldn't avoid rather than someone they couldn't stop thinking about. But I've seen people falling in love...'

'And?'

'And they're nauseating. Always touching, always looking for each other or at each other or deeply into one another's eyes.' For all her humour there was a wistfulness in Maddie's voice that spoke to Dante, a yearning he understood all too well. A yearning to be understood, to be wanted, to be loved.

A yearning he never intended to fill again. That want was all too seductive—and couldn't be trusted.

'Not everyone.'

'No, and of course we are trying to be discreet.' Maddie turned and took a step closer to him. She was a tall woman and the heels she wore added another two inches to her height, but Dante could still look down onto the top of her golden head—until, that was, she looked up at him and he was lost in the grey depths of her eyes. Were those silver flecks he could see?

'Discreet,' Dante agreed, not capable of doing much more than parroting the word. How could one step make such a difference—one step and a glance? One moment they had been standing side by side in a perfectly calm way, having a perfectly rational conversation—and yes, he had noticed how attractive she was; he was still in the prime of life after all. And yes, he had discovered that he liked Madeleine Fitzroy, admired her sense of humour and obvious intelligence, despite her taste in music and food, and *that*, considering the week they had ahead of them, was all to the good. But now he couldn't tear his eyes away from her upturned face, his gaze moving with difficulty from hers, only to stutter to a stop as he reached the pink lushness of her mouth. Now the attraction had cranked up a gear or ten and Dante suddenly found it hard to catch his breath.

'But your sister is going to be looking for those signs that even discreet people can't help displaying. The looks, the odd touches here and there. The kisses.' Her mouth parted on the last word and Dante swayed forward, just a little, like a bee scenting nectar.

Maddie's scent enveloped him, floral with hints of citrus adding a refreshing bite. He was almost dizzy with the intoxicating scent, with the pink of her mouth, with her nearness.

'That complicates things a little.' Now it was his turn to take a step closer, so close they were almost—almost—touching. So close he knew another millimetre would bring their bodies into alignment. 'I think we need to be prepared.'

'Prepared?' Now she was the one repeating his words to him and when Dante dragged his gaze back to meet hers he couldn't help but feel a primal satisfaction at the glazed look in her eyes, at the way her tongue darted over her plump lips, the way she swayed ever nearer...

'We should practise. Looking like we're falling in love. Maybe with a little touching...' and he ran one finger lightly down her cheek and along the silken line of her mouth. Maddie's eyes fluttered shut and it took all Dante's resolve not to pull her to him, crush her against him and taste her.

But this was a business contract and, for all the pheromones clouding the air, for all his blood was thundering around his body, it had to be a meeting in the middle. One step by him, one step by her, mutually agreeable terms.

'That makes sense,' Maddie breathed, leaning her cheek against his touch like a cat seeking adulation. 'Practice makes perfect after all.' She slipped her arm around his waist, her hand splaying on his back, and Dante could feel the imprint of every finger clearly through the thin cotton of his shirt. Slowly, so slowly it took everything he had not to groan, she raised herself on tiptoe and pressed one light, teasing kiss on his mouth.

Dante froze at the warm contact, as electricity zapped straight through him. What was he doing? He'd known this girl had fire the second they had connected across the lake and yet here he was, allowing himself to be burned, allowing her heat to melt the ice that encased him and kept him safe.

He should step back; their point was well and truly made. They needed to remember to act like lovers.

But was there any real difference between acting like lovers and *being* lovers? When they both knew the score?

'Maybe we should practise a little more.' Was that his voice? So ragged? So hoarse? Dante didn't want to think, to dwell, to analyse a moment longer. Instead he stepped back, away from her touch and slowly, deliberately, walked behind Maddie, sweeping her long length of hair aside. He took his time, kissing his way down the column of her throat, savouring the tang of her skin, exultation running through him as she leaned against him, a sigh escaping her parted lips. His hands moved to her bare shoulders, his fingertips running up and down her upper arms, enjoying the feel of her skin under his.

'You taste so good,' he whispered in her ear and felt her shiver at his words.

'Dante, I…' She captured his hands with hers and turned, eyes luminous in the approaching twilight. 'I can't. Not here. Not on the deck. Anyone could walk up at any time.'

She was right. He should signal to the captain to turn the boat around, to make their way back to shore, drive her back to her apartment, drop her off and then do his best to sleep this intoxication off. He should—and he would. If that was what she wanted. '*Si*. Of course…' He swallowed, knowing he was too close to making himself vulnerable. 'There's a suite. On the boat. We don't have to return to shore until I say. Until you say. If you want…'

'A suite?'

'Just a few steps away.'

Maddie smiled then, soft and seductive and yet a little shy. 'Then what are we waiting for? I believe we have a lot more practising to do yet, *signor*.'

CHAPTER SIX

MADDIE COULD HARDLY believe her own daring as she allowed Dante to take her hand and lead her down the short staircase into the boat's interior. She, Madeleine Fitzroy, had never, ever engaged in this kind of impulsive, wild behaviour before. There had been nothing urgent or desperate about her past relationships—they hadn't been unpleasant, but the best word to describe her past experiences was 'nice'. At twenty-six she was more than ready to graduate from nice to amazing.

And somehow she sensed tonight was the night.

Maybe it was the way every touch made her shiver. Maybe it was the gleam of intent in Dante's cool blue gaze. Maybe it was the curve of his mouth and the promise inherent in his smile. Maybe it was the deep yearning low in her stomach, a sweet ache in her breasts, a need to touch and be touched that was so strong it overpowered any other thought.

Or maybe it was because Dante was right when he had accused her of hiding. Maddie had left her home, her country, everything she knew in order to reinvent herself. But getting on the flight had been the limit of her impulsiveness. Once she had reached Italy she had hidden behind a laptop for ten months, living vicariously through other people's dreams and hopes and desires. No more.

She needed to reach for what she wanted. No more sleeping through her own life like the sloths she was so desperate to see. No more allowing other people to make decisions for her, going along with the status quo because it was safe and easy and she knew her role was to keep things smooth. No more pouring all her desire and passion into ancient buildings that didn't even belong to her and would still be standing long after she was gone. No. She wanted an adventure, right? Well, she was starting right here. Right now.

Being adventurous—*being* an adventuress.

She barely noticed the short corridor, all her focus on the feel of Dante's hand in hers, the breadth of his shoulders, the promise in his stride. They reached a polished wood door and Dante opened it, gesturing her inside. 'I am just going to call the captain and ask him to sail and dock in Desenzano—if that's all right with you. The staff all live near there. They can return in the morning and sail us back to Riva.'

Maddie turned at that. 'They won't mind if we stay on board?'

'Why would they?' Dante raised an eyebrow. 'The boat belongs to me. Paolo, the captain, and his nephew work for me full-time.'

He kept a fully staffed boat on Lake Garda even though he stayed in the region for just a couple of months every year? Just how rich was Dante Falcone? Money didn't impress Maddie—after all, one of her cousins owned a good third of Scotland and another had married an oil tycoon and lived in the kind of lavish luxury last seen in an eighties soap opera. Maddie herself had been brought up in the kind of aristocratic gentility that found an excess of money a little vulgar. But despite herself she couldn't help being a little impressed by the extravagance.

Dante strode over to an intercom panel on the wall and after pressing a button began to speak in low, rapid Italian. Maddie took a deep breath, taking advantage of his momentary distraction to look around at her surroundings—and to clear her head a little.

Maddie hadn't been on many boats before; those she had been on had certainly been comfortable, bordering on luxurious—but they didn't compare to this. Dante had brought her into a suite to rival any five-star hotel. She stood in a sumptuously outfitted sitting room, the dark wood of the polished floor echoed by the panelling on the walls. The outside wall was all glass, offering breathtaking views out onto the sunset-lit lake beyond. A vast white sofa curved around, facing a cinema-style screen on the wall, the screen flanked by recessed bookshelves. A glossy desk took up the corner, the laptop already set up, showing this was a place where Dante came to work as well as play.

The door behind the sofa was half-open and Maddie could see an equally big room, this one dominated by a huge bed. She swallowed at the sight of it. She wasn't in this room for a tour of the boat's interior. She was down here because of that bed. Her legs were suddenly a little wobbly, her palms dampening at the realisation. Could she really be about to spend the night with a man she barely knew?

'Second thoughts?'

She jumped as Dante's low voice reverberated through her. She hadn't heard him walk up behind her.

'No... I...' But of *course* she was having second thoughts. Maddie so desperately wanted to be someone else, someone new, but making the jump was so much harder than she had anticipated.

And yet...the one time she had been really impulsive, the one time she had listened to the screaming of her heart, not the sensible drum in her head, she had called off her wedding. She hadn't cared about the scandal, or the 'spectacle' she had made of herself—according to her mother. She had just gone with everything her body and her soul were telling her. And it had been absolutely the right thing to do.

'Maddie. It's fine. We can...'

Reaching up, Maddie laid one finger on Dante's lips and watched with satisfaction as he swallowed, his pupils dilating at her touch. 'We can what? You're not backing out on me, are you, Conte Falcone?'

'No.' The low word was almost a growl, igniting a fire in Maddie's belly as Dante stepped close, one hand slipping around to caress the nape of her neck. Maddie shivered as his skilled fingers brushed her skin, the memory of his kisses in that very spot still reverberating through her body. He brushed his other hand down her cheek and she closed her eyes to better lose herself in the gentle caress, swaying closer, her whole body aching in anticipation until finally—finally—his mouth descended on hers and she fell willingly and wholly into his embrace.

His kiss was soft—at first—tantalising Maddie with the promise of heat. Emboldened, she finally allowed her hands to explore the muscles and planes of his back and torso, skimming over his shirt, searching for a way through the cloth frustrating her need for skin on skin. His own touch remained provokingly light, one hand caressing her neck, the other at her waist, his fingers stroking from the curve of her hip to the bottom of her ribcage but no further. Maddie's breasts ached with the need for that touch to reach them and with a low moan she pressed herself closer, grabbing Dante's shirt to pull it out of his waistband, purring with satisfaction as she finally felt hot skin under her fingertips. With a primal satisfaction she felt him quiver at her touch, heard his breathing speed up as his kiss intensified. Maddie held on as tight as she could, losing herself in heat, in sensation, in want and need. She had never felt like this before. This wild, this uninhibited. She wanted to touch, to taste him everywhere; she didn't want him to stop touching her.

She was barely conscious of their movement as Dante, still kissing her as if she was the most desirable woman in the world, slowly walked her through the door into the bedroom. The large bed was no longer intimidating; it was exactly what she wanted, what she needed. Dante was who she wanted, who she needed. They had one night. She intended to make the most of every single moment.

'Morning, sleepyhead.'

Maddie stirred, opening one eye to see sunlight streaming in through the window. With a shock she realised she hadn't been aware when they had docked, when the crew had left. All she had known was sensation and moans and desire.

She automatically reached up and smoothed her hair, desperately trying to think of the right expression to say *'Well, thank you for a lovely evening and a rather sensational night; now let's never speak about it again because if I have to work with you and remember the things you did to me—and the way I responded—I may never be able to look you in the eye again'.*

'Morning,' she said instead.

'I've been out and got you a coffee and some pastries. Your phone has been buzzing away as well.' Dante put a cup of coffee and a bag filled with tiny, flaky pastries onto the bedside table and dropped Maddie's phone onto the bed.

'Thank you.' She sat up slowly, one hand gripping the sheet, making sure it covered as much of her as possible. The problem with being adventurous was that she hadn't bought any night things, any spare underwear—all she had was a strappy silver dress. If Dante drove her back to the castle, make-up smeared under her eyes, hair tangled and in that dress, she might as well hang a banner from her window that said 'Yes. I slept with my boss'.

The coffee smelt amazing but Maddie reached for her phone first, her stomach churning as she saw the furiously flashing light which denoted messages. Her fingers were clumsy as she tried several times to unlock her screen with her fingerprint, giving up and punching her code in instead, smothering a curse as she mistyped the numbers, eventually managing to bring up her messages. Ten missed calls, as many emails, all flagged important. Wiggling the sheet a little further up her body, she pressed 'voicemail', all too aware of Dante leaning against the wall, watching her.

The tension ratcheted up as she heard Guido's excited tone, only to dissipate as his words sank in. Easing back on her pillows, she listened to the rest of her messages then quickly checked her emails.

'Everything okay?'

'Kind of. Tomorrow's guests aren't coming. They've called the wedding off.' Her voice wavered a little on the last word, memories of the manically unreal days after her own curtailed wedding resurfacing. 'Better now than later, I suppose. Don't worry. They've paid in full and there are no refunds at this stage.'

'So what does this mean for you?'

'I need to make sure everything they ordered has been cancelled. We don't need the ornate flower sculptures or the band or any of the excursions now. That's just a couple of hours' work though. It doesn't have much effect on me or the castle staff, apart from making this week a little easier, I suppose. I'll be answering queries from booked-in and prospective brides as usual, but we're all ready for the rest of the summer. All the food and decorations for the next couple of months have been agreed on and ordered, excursions booked in...' Her voice trailed off. Maddie was so used to juggling the dual demands of catering to the wedding party currently in situ with the organising for future brides that she wasn't sure how she would fill her time without half her workload.

'So you'll have some spare time?'

'Possibly,' Maddie agreed cautiously. 'Why?'

Dante's grin was pure wolf. 'Looks like you'll be earning that bonus and plane ticket after all. You can use those hostessing skills of yours to help me persuade my sister that I am more than capable of looking after myself so that, even when you've left and I have to admit to her that I am single once again, she won't worry about me or try and set me up with her friends.'

'I...'

But of course she had agreed to this proposition already and without work as a buffer there was no reason for her not to spend more time with Luciana—and by extension with Dante. 'Of course,' she agreed with as much dignity as was possible when she was wearing nothing but a sheet.

It was one thing to wear a sheet when they were both in similar stages of undress, but quite another when Dante was fully dressed—not in the formal shirt and trousers he had worn last night but the most casual clothes she had seen him in to date. Black jeans skimmed his hips before hugging powerful thighs in a way that made her muscles clench in physical memory of just how strong his legs were. He'd teamed the jeans with a soft grey T-shirt, the stubble on his chin combining with the relaxed clothes to give him a sexy morning vibe almost as intoxicating as the smartly dressed intensity of the evening before.

'Excellent. I'm picking Luciana up from Verona later today. Why don't we head there this morning and spend the day sightseeing before we meet her train?'

Why don't we *what*?

'I don't really have the right clothes for sightseeing. I wasn't expecting this.'

This was the best euphemism she could think of for the night they had shared, and her current state of undress. Dante's suggestion of a day together went well beyond their agreed parameters. But it was a suggestion Maddie was surprisingly keen to agree to, despite at least a hundred reasons why it was a bad idea. She fumbled for those reasons, not sure if she was trying to get out of the day or if she wanted Dante to talk her around. 'And I really need to get those cancellations done this morning. Besides, doesn't Arianna want to meet her aunt?'

Never over-egg with three excuses when you only need one. Dante's grin just grew a little more wolfish as Maddie talked on and he folded his arms as she finished, the picture of relaxed ease.

'The laptop on the desk is configured to the Falcone network, so after you have eaten your breakfast you can send all your emails easily. Meanwhile, I can go and purchase anything you need for the day. As for Arianna, she has made friends with a girl her age in San Tomo and has been invited to spend the day swimming with her and begged me to excuse her. Anything else?'

Yes! My agreement is to pretend to your sister that we are in a relationship, not to spend the day in Verona— Verona, for goodness' sake, city of romance and doomed love—sightseeing after the best night of my life!

Maddie hitched the sheet a little higher. Any higher and it would be a veil. She felt a little like the grandma peering out at the big bad wolf, unsure whether he was going to eat her up or not. And half wanting him to...

'We could go back to Riva and then head to Verona later to pick up your sister if that's easier.'

'We could, but you have never been to Verona. It's just a forty-minute drive from here, so why not take advantage of the opportunity to see it?'

'I agree it makes sense, but won't it complicate things?'

The look Dante shot her was bland. 'Complicate?'

'After last night.'

'It wasn't just last night,' he said softly and Maddie's body heated so quickly she was sure a neon glow could be seen shining through the sheet. 'I seem to remember this morning too...'

Dante watched Maddie with amusement. Last night's confident siren had faded away, the cool, poised, professional woman gone, replaced with an adorably confused and even more adorably tousled girl hiding behind a sheet, cheeks aflame.

'Maddie,' he said, low and coaxingly. All he wanted to do was stride over to the bed, take the phone from her hand and kiss her until all the doubts melted from her eyes. But that kind of persuasion wasn't in their agreement. Nor was he going to give in to that kind of instinct, that kind of lust and need and want.

But it still took everything he had to stay leaning against the wall, to keep his body relaxed, his face neutral. 'We can, of course, return to the *castello* if that's what you prefer. But the fates have gifted you with a week off. Why not take advantage of their kindness?'

'I'm just not sure spending any more time alone together is a good idea.'

'I see. You think we've had enough practice? Last night was enough?'

'Yes; no, I… Last night was amazing, but today I… Oh! See?' She sat up and glared indignantly at him. 'This is what I mean about complicating things.'

'Madeleine. It's only complicated if we let it be.' *Liar*, his body whispered.

'I know. The problem is…' She paused. 'Look. I wanted to—you know—last night. I've wanted to since that first day—and you have as well,' she added defiantly.

Dante didn't deny it—couldn't deny it. *'Si.'*

'So what now? What do we do all week? Pretend it didn't happen? Admit it did and chalk it up to a learning experience and be more careful next time? Or…?'

Dante was voting for *or*, whatever 'or' might turn out to be. 'I think you might be overthinking things, *cara*.'

The endearment slipped out before he could curb it. But luckily Maddie didn't seem to have noticed it. 'Maybe. I just want to know where we stand.'

'Maddie. You are a beautiful woman. We spent a very nice evening together, enjoying each other's company. We will be spending a great deal of time together this week, pretending that we are falling in love. Why not just enjoy the ride?'

She bit her lip and Dante couldn't tear his eyes away from the plump flesh, the neat indentation of her lip. 'You make it sound so easy.'

'That's because it is. By the end of the summer I will be back in Roma, you will be cuddling small bears covered in mould and these days will be just a memory. Why not make them a nice memory? And so here we are. With a beautiful day ahead of us. Where shall we spend it? Back in the *castello*, or shall we set our scene in fair Verona?'

'Don't misquote Shakespeare; it's not as if Romeo and Juliet ended that well.' But Maddie smiled as she spoke, her grip on the sheet loosening, allowing it to slip down, unveiling her graceful neck, her slim shoulders.

'Ah, but we're just playing at lovers. That makes us completely safe. And just to make sure, I promise that, no matter how annoying your cousin, I won't murder him in the street.'

'That's a load off my mind. I don't actually like my cousins all that much, but I'd rather they weren't slaughtered in a duel. So we just see where things take us? I can do that.' Maddie reached for her coffee and the bag of pastries, her eyes brightening as she peeked inside at the selection he had chosen. She selected a simple *cornetto* before holding the bag out to him. 'Okay, *signor*. You're right. It would be lovely to see Verona. Thank you.'

Dante managed not to react as the tension left his body. He didn't want to think too much about just why it had mattered that Maddie had agreed that this brief affair could continue. Better to settle on the reason that the week ahead would be much easier if they were physically comfortable with each other. Or remember that it had been nearly a year since his last discreet affair and surely he was due another.

'Why don't you shower and sort out your emails and I will go and purchase whatever you need for the day ahead?' he suggested.

'Really? You don't mind buying me underwear?' Maddie asked through a mouthful of crumbs.

'Why would I? I have a daughter, after all. I am an expert in how to braid her hair in at least five different ways, I have talked to her about growing up and adolescence, am ready to sit and rub her back and feed her ice cream when she gets her first period—buying you some mascara and tights really doesn't come close to the panic I felt when Arianna first asked me about how babies are made.'

'I bet you're a wonderful father.'

'I do the best I can.' He could never make up for the fact his daughter was motherless. Never forgive himself for his blindness, for dismissing Violetta's unhappiness, for allowing himself to live in a daydream rather than reality. But he had sworn on the day he'd buried his wife that his daughter wouldn't suffer for his folly. That he would be father and mother both, that she would always come first. And she did. Even though she had an au pair, Dante still did as many school drop-offs as possible, picked her up whenever he could. He sat in ballet school waiting rooms and cheered on the side of football fields, he watched films about princesses and films about spaceships and films about talking dogs, read to her every night he was home and, yes, his braiding skills were now legendary amongst Arianna's friends. 'Write me a list of what you need and I'll be as quick as I can.'

'Thank you, Dante.' Maddie had barely called him by his given name and an unexpected thrill ran through him at the precise syllables. 'For everything, for making this so easy. For last night. I never... It was never like that before.'

Dante froze. The truth was it had never been like that for him either, not even in those first heady days of infatuation with Violetta. Never been so sweet, so all-consuming. But he didn't want to dwell on why that might be—or make himself vulnerable in any way. 'No need to thank me.' His smile was purposefully intimate. 'I enjoyed myself too.'

Her answering smile matched his, elegant brows arching in a question. 'Oh? That's good to hear. I was thinking...' Maddie's voice trailed off suggestively.

'Yes?'

'Well, if you don't have to rush off then maybe we could practise a little more. Just to make sure we haven't forgotten anything.'

'You are a very conscientious woman, Signorina Fitzroy,' Dante told her as he walked purposefully towards her, unbuttoning his shirt, aware of Maddie's gaze fixed on his every move. 'Amazing attention to detail.'

'I try,' she whispered, her chest rising and falling with her shallow breaths.

'I agree it's wise to make sure we didn't forget anything. After all, didn't we agree that practice makes perfect?' And as he sank onto the bed, enveloped by her scent, her arms, her need, Dante couldn't help but think he was willing to practise for as long as it took.

CHAPTER SEVEN

'I CAN'T BELIEVE it's taken me nearly a year to come here,' Maddie said wistfully as she slowly turned a full three hundred and sixty degrees. They were standing in the Teatro Romano looking out over the ancient city of Verona. 'It's so beautiful—and so different from San Tomo. It seems incredible that it's so close.' Instead of lakes and mountains, here were rivers and hills, Roman ruins interspersed with medieval houses and newer builds, the ages merging into one beautiful whole.

'I never thought that I would need to scold one of my employees for working too hard,' Dante teased her. 'But in your case, *signorina*, I make an exception.'

'I send my wedding parties here all the time, suggest places for them to go, book tickets for the opera, but have never thought that maybe I should come along as well.'

'You like the opera?'

'I'm not sure,' she admitted. 'I've been to Glyndebourne of course, but it was always more of a social occasion than a musical one.' She held her hands up, laughing at the look of horror on Dante's face. 'I know, I'm a philistine.'

'I will get us tickets for the festival here,' he said firmly.

'You don't have to...'

'Luciana will want to go. Consider it part of your duties as well as your education.'

'Education and work in one outing? Fabulous.'

But despite her words she couldn't help the tingle of anticipation at the idea. Not just because she would get the opportunity to view one of the most famous cultural events in the world, but because Dante wanted her to experience something he loved.

And from someone so private that was a heady thought indeed.

Not that the cool and proper Conte had been much in evidence today. After they finally resurfaced from the bed, Dante had headed back out into the town to purchase Maddie a suitable outfit for the day. Even after the night they had shared she'd felt a little embarrassed scribbling her demands—and her sizes—down, but he had brushed her concerns and her offer of payment aside, returning with something really pretty and expensive, judging by the cut, blue-silk maxi-dress covered in a gorgeous flowery pattern. He'd teamed the dress with dull gold sandals and a matching scarf, also supplying her with exquisitely beautiful lace underwear that Maddie thought ruefully must have cost more than all her sensible sets of bras and pants put together. Luckily she carried a few essential travel cosmetics in her bag, so she'd managed to powder her nose and tame her hair before he returned. After reassuring both Guido and the distraught bride that everything was in hand, she had spent a busy hour ensuring everything that could be cancelled was.

At least by waiting until she'd got to the altar to call off her own wedding she hadn't had to do anything except cancel the honeymoon. The bemused guests had been invited to stay and enjoy the food and music and, in the end, most of them had. Maddie herself had danced until midnight—hence the photo which had appeared in most of the papers of a bride alone on a dance floor in full white dress and tiara. The first time she had ever just *been*, without caring what anyone thought. The first and last time—until last night.

Dante had driven them to Verona in the same car he had transported her down the mountainside in last night. Maddie hadn't asked how the car had miraculously appeared at the other end of the lake. She was beginning to realise that the *castello* was just a very small part of the Falcone empire and fortune. Which made Dante's determination to make his sister happy just that little bit more endearing.

Endearing—not a word she'd expected to use about the Conte. And not, considering both the tenor of their agreement and the way she'd thrown caution overboard last night, a word she needed to be using. Endearing was too friendly, too sweet a word.

A little like the day they were spending together. It was both sweet and friendly—but with an edge. An awareness of each other that stayed with them every step, every touch. Every time Dante spoke, Maddie remembered the way his mouth felt on hers, on her body, remembered the endearments he had whispered in the dark of the night. Every time their hands briefly touched she had flashbacks to the way he had touched her last night. A reminder that this was no normal day. It was a prologue to the real business, the real reason they were spending any time together at all.

'And so,' Dante said as they finally reached the top of the theatre and gazed down at Verona spread before them, unreal in its beauty and antiquity, 'there she is. Verona in all her glory.'

'Glorious,' Maddie murmured, every nerve ablaze with awareness of Dante's proximity. Her body swayed towards him, yearning for his touch. Part of her gloried in this new sensation, in the abandonment he had induced in her—but part of her shrank from it. Maddie was no prude, she wasn't naïve, but she had assumed— she had hoped—that if she ever felt this kind of passion then it would be accompanied by love, not something as prosaic as a business contract. She knew Dante found her attractive. But he'd said very clearly that he didn't want a relationship with anyone. That he didn't believe in love.

Whereas Maddie believed wholeheartedly in love. She just wasn't sure she'd ever find anyone who loved her. After all, she never had. Oh, she knew her parents would tell her not to be so silly, so sentimental, that of course they loved her. But it was a love balanced by approval, by doing the right thing, by conforming. Every time she broke out of the established mould—even when it was for their benefit—she felt them pull away.

She wanted to be loved no matter what.

Dante's voice broke into her thoughts and she pulled herself back into the present. How spoiled she was! She was having a perfectly lovely day—after a perfectly lovely night. What else did a young, free woman need? 'What would you like to do next?'

There was only one possible answer. They'd walked along the river, crossed the gorgeously crenulated Ponte di Castel Vecchio and admired the castle itself. They'd wandered through the various piazzas, stopping off for coffees and a long lunch along the way, before spending a restful hour in the Giardino Gusti, glad of the shade in the heat of the summer's afternoon. Now they had nearly two hours before meeting Luciana's train and there was one key destination they had yet to visit.

'I know it isn't authentic…' she began and Dante interrupted.

'Of course,' he said resignedly. 'Bring a girl to Verona and she has to stand in an overcrowded courtyard to stare at a balcony which was added long after the date the supposed occupant of the house used it, to pay homage to a pair of teenagers with chronic communication issues.'

'It wasn't their fault. They didn't exactly have smartphones in the fourteenth century.' Maddie didn't know why she was defending a pair of fictional characters so vehemently. But standing here in Verona, where the fourteenth century didn't just seem relevant but practically modern while she was surrounded by Roman ruins, Romeo and Juliet seemed less like people in a play and more like the embodiment of hope and dreams. Even if it had all gone famously wrong.

'One moment Romeo is sighing over Rosaline and the next he's falling for Juliet. If Juliet hadn't been a Capulet and they hadn't rushed into marriage, who knows who he would have fallen for next? As for Juliet… She should have listened to her mother and married Paris. These mad passions don't last,' he finished, a hint of bitterness penetrating the irony.

'That would have made a fascinating play. And of course,' Maddie answered sweetly, 'I forgot how sensibly everyone always behaves in opera. Lots of sitting around discussing things rationally over tea and cake.'

'It's the music that makes the opera, not the story.'

'Not true—it's passionate music inspired by passionate characters. And it's the same in Shakespeare; the language is what moves us, what makes the story. After all, Shakespeare recycled most of the stories.'

Dante sighed in the long-suffering way of one who already knew the answer to a question about to be asked. 'So, knowing that neither Romeo nor Juliet have ever been proved to actually exist and also that the balcony is a later addition, would you still like to go?'

'Absolutely. Consider it an advance payment for the opera.'

Dante muttered something that sounded more than a little like 'philistine' but didn't demur any more; instead he took Maddie's arm in a surprisingly pleasant proprietorial gesture and guided her down the steps. Maddie was more than capable of walking down a set of stone steps, even if they were two thousand years old and a little unsteady in places, but it was nice to find herself being taken care of rather than the person doing the caring.

Nice and novel.

It was about half a mile's stroll to the famous balcony, crossing back across the river and making their way through the cobbled streets until they finally reached the small courtyard thronged with people. Greenery covered the high walls on one side and it was easy to imagine a youthful lover climbing up it to reach his lady-love. Maddie shivered despite the heat, despite the crowds chattering in at least a dozen languages. To be loved so desperately, to be wanted so intensely that you would rather die than be separated. Melodramatic? Sure. But also so intoxicatingly sweet. A sweetness every fibre in her body yearned for. Last night had been incredible, mind-blowingly, fantastically incredible, but instead of fulfilling a need it had just opened up the chasm inside her heart a little wider. Maddie didn't just want good sex, lovely as that was—really lovely; she wanted love. Not because of how she made someone's life easier but because of who she was. She wanted someone to see inside her and love and desire all of her.

Who would have thought the sensible Honourable Madeleine Fitzroy would turn out to be such a romantic? It certainly wasn't from her upbringing. None of her ancestors had a romantic bone in their body, the Bryon-worshipping, gothic-folly-building nineteenth-century would-be rake aside, and he wasn't so much romantic as a *romantic*. He had yearned for adventure and daring deeds of valour rather than love.

Her mother would probably prescribe a long dog walk and a cup of cocoa. Her father would pat her on the head and tell her—remind her—that she was a good girl. If Juliet had been a Fitzroy she would have married Paris, just as Dante had said, knowing her duty and doing it obediently. But if she had wavered, had allowed herself to follow her heart and woken up in that tomb with her dead swain lying across her, poison bottle clasped in his still warm hand, then would she have died for love or would she have allowed herself one solitary tear and then got on with her dutiful life, only occasionally allowing herself to remember her entombed lover?

Maddie suspected the latter.

But at least Juliet would have lived out her life knowing that she had once been loved to the point of madness. Would Maddie ever know the same? She'd take a week of wild passion over a lifetime of duty any day. Otherwise she might as well have married Theo.

'Would you like to go inside the house? There's a mu-

seum, I believe.' Dante's voice broke into her reverie and
Maddie pulled herself back into reality.

'No, thank you. This is great. Look at all these people.
I wonder what they're thinking?'

Tour parties, young couples kissing under the balcony,
lone sightseers, families with fractious toddlers or sulky
teens, older couples holding hands... All of humanity
seemed to be represented in the square.

'That it's too busy in here and they want a coffee—or
better still a glass of wine?'

'They're not thinking about coffee,' Maddie said wistfully, her gaze drawn to a couple around her age who
were staring into each other's eyes as if nobody else existed. At that moment the young man dropped to his knee
and presented a box to his blushing girlfriend. 'Oh, my
goodness—look, Dante. How romantic. A proposal. Oh,
thank goodness she said yes. Can you imagine how embarrassing it would have been if she hadn't? Oh, what a
romantic place to choose.'

'A busy square full of tourists?' His voice was full of
cynicism and Maddie's heart ached for him. He'd told her
he'd been besotted with his wife—how had that young
man full of love and hope turned so bitter?

'It might not be the most private place, but it shows
some imagination.' Maddie sighed. 'When Theo asked
me to marry him we had just got out of the car and were
walking towards the back door at Flintock Hall. It was
slippery underfoot, thanks to the frost, and I was so busy
trying to make sure I didn't fall I didn't hear what he
said. It was part of a longer speech about how grateful
he was for all I did, and how we had known each other
all our lives and how much he respected me. No wonder I didn't hear the "wouldn't it make a lot of sense if

we got married?" part.' She smiled as she watched the couple enthusiastically embrace in the midst of a circle of well-wishers. 'I'm not one for public displays of affection or for overly complicated proposals, but if anyone ever proposes to me again I want romance and heart. Not that it seems likely right now. You're the first man I've kissed in over a year—and we're all about business.'

'Not *all* about business,' Dante said softly and Maddie felt the increasingly familiar heat flush through her at his words.

'Okay, maybe not *all* about business. But not all about romance either. Don't worry,' she added hurriedly. 'I'm not asking you to suddenly start buying me roses and to serenade me under a balcony. I would just like to know that one day I will fall in love with someone who loves me. Just the basics really.'

'People used to write love notes and stick them on the walls, but that is now strictly forbidden. But they say that if you touch the statue of Juliet,' Dante grinned, slow and dangerous, 'specifically her right breast, then that will bring good fortune in love.'

'Really?' Maddie looked over at the bronze statue doubtfully. 'That seems a little over-familiar. Poor Juliet. I don't think she signed up to be groped by a bunch of strangers.'

'Maddie. It's a statue.'

'You think I should do it?'

'I think it's nonsense. The statue, the superstition and romance. All of it. But you don't, so here you are. What harm can it do?'

Maddie chewed on her lip. On the one hand the very idea seemed embarrassing. To touch a statue—and so intimately—and signal to the world that she was lonely and looking for love. On the other hand she had promised herself she would be open to new experiences. To stop worrying about how people perceived her. To relax and enjoy life. Dante was right; she was already here. Why not join all the other tourists, none of whom seemed to give touching the statue a second thought?

Besides. She *did* want love. She wasn't in a position to turn down any chance to increase her luck, no matter how unlikely it seemed.

'Okay, then.' She lifted her chin and gave Dante as jaunty a grin as she could manage. 'Wish me luck.'

Dante leaned against the wall and watched Maddie as she approached the statue, head back and shoulders as taut as if she was heading into battle—which in some ways she was. Not just because she had to get past the other people vying to caress the statue, but because she was setting out her stall and asking the universe for love.

His body tensed. Part of him wanted to pull her away and warn her that she was heading for nowhere but heartbreak and loneliness. Tell her that she should have gone through with her wedding because respect and similar goals were the best foundations he could think of to build a marriage and a family on.

But part of him wanted to applaud her courage. Wished he had her ability to hope and believe.

Though he had to ask the question—what the hell were British men thinking? How on earth had someone as sexy and intelligent and interesting as Maddie ended up thinking she needed a statue's help to find love? She should have been snapped up years ago, not allowed to measure her worth through her name and her ability to run a large estate.

She gave him a quick, almost flirtatious glance over her shoulder and Dante gave her a thumbs-up as she reached out and almost reverentially placed her palm on the statue, her hand flat on the side of Juliet's breast. Maddie closed her eyes and murmured something Dante couldn't make out before stepping back and relinquishing her place to the next eager tourist who, Dante noted disapprovingly, didn't treat the Shakespearian heroine with the respect she deserved.

'So?' He straightened as she neared him. 'Feel any different?'

'Oh, yes, the world is full of opportunities. Any second now one of these men is going to fall to his knees before me and profess his undying love.'

'I hope they won't mind waiting a week,' Dante said drily. 'You are otherwise engaged, after all.' It wasn't jealousy or ownership that prompted him to take her hand. He really had no need to be jealous and he had no desire to have any claim on her. He just wanted to ensure he didn't lose her in the crowd as they exited the bustling square. But he had to admit, the softness of her hand in his felt—well, it felt nice. Right.

'Thank you.'

He looked at her enquiringly.

'For suggesting today. I've had a really good time.'

'Me too.' And he had. 'It's been too long since I've been here. Violetta preferred La Scala to the festival; she liked going to the opera to see and be seen, not for the music. She preferred the shopping in Milan. The couple of times we came here she got bored quickly. She would want to shop and to lunch and that was that.'

'In that case, maybe I shouldn't mention that I was hoping we'd have time to browse in a couple of the book-shops we passed?' Maddie shot him a quick, apologetic glance. 'Don't worry about it. Now I've ventured here I'm pretty sure it won't be my last visit. It's just so beautiful. So much history in one place.'

She wanted to go to a bookstore? Not to a designer dress shop, or one of the many luxury bag or shoe shops, or the expensive make-up stores? She didn't want to browse the jewellery counters? That was the only type of sightseeing Violetta had enjoyed, and she would always return laden with bags, despite wardrobes full of unworn clothes at home. It wasn't that Dante had begrudged spending a penny on his wife—the opposite. He had adored lavishing gifts on her. It was just that, no matter what he had bought her, it was never enough. It never made her happy—*he* never made her happy. And, in truth, she hadn't made him happy either. She had never tried to enjoy his interests or wanted to spend time on the things he liked doing and by the time he had realised how little they had in common it was too late. In the end he had come to the opera alone, come to explore the ruins alone, peruse the bookstores alone. He'd been alone long before he was bereaved. He just had never admitted it.

Luckily he knew better now. Knew that loneliness wasn't something to fear; rather it was a safety to embrace. A timely reminder on a day when the personal and business were melding together in a way he hadn't expected, on a day when he found himself relaxing his guard. A day when, for one moment, watching Maddie touch the statue, he had hoped all her dreams came true and wished he could be the man to do that for her. A foolish wish—better he wish that she was never disillusioned. That if love came it was kinder to her than it had been to him.

'A bookstore? Of course, Verona is famed for its book-shops,' he said and Maddie beamed.

'Good! I've read all the English books at the *castello* several times over—and my written Italian is by no means as fluent as my spoken.' She was still chattering as they reached the first shop, only stopping when she took in the shelves of books, her mouth falling open in awe.

'Go, browse,' Dante told her. 'We still have time.'

'I never want to leave this place,' she said solemnly, heading towards the English section as if she were drawn there by the Pied Piper.

Dante stood and watched her, noting the reverential way she selected a book, the way she was instantly absorbed as she read it, and was conscious of a nostalgic longing for the young man who would once have lost himself in dreams as she did. He turned hurriedly, wanting, needing to break the connection and his gaze fell on a table of journals. Diaries, recipe books, travel writings. He picked up a gorgeously embellished travel journal, remembering the light in Maddie's eyes as she had talked him through her plans. A light he had wanted to bathe in, even as his heart twisted at the knowledge that her plans involved being a long way from him.

No. He should be glad for her—and relieved for himself. She was leaving at the end of the summer—and that made her safe. As long as he remembered that she was leaving, as long as he remembered that ultimately she wanted what he could no longer give, then he was safe.

And safety was all that mattered.

CHAPTER EIGHT

'WHERE DO I PRESS?'

'Right there. That's it.' Maddie shifted slightly. For a small, skinny child, Arianna seemed to weigh an awful lot, especially when all her weight was on just one knee. 'And then press there and there… That's it! You've just finalised a booking.'

'All by myself?'

'All by yourself,' Maddie confirmed, smiling at the child's evident glee. 'You're a natural. I'll have to be careful or I'll find myself out of a job.'

'What's this? You're not annoying Maddie, are you, *piccola*?'

They both jumped at the sound of Dante's voice and Maddie swung the chair round, noting with a slight feeling of guilt the flare of surprise in his eyes as he noted Arianna on her knee. They had agreed to be extra careful with each other around Arianna and ensure that Luciana said nothing either, but when Arianna had shown up in Maddie's office that morning, she hadn't been able to bring herself to send the small girl away; something in her eagerness to learn—and the wistful loneliness in her eyes—struck a nostalgic chord. Besides, Maddie reasoned, as far as Arianna knew, Maddie was nothing but an employee, so what harm could letting her hang around do?

To her surprise she was enjoying Arianna's company. Maddie had never spent much time with children before, had always found herself unsure what to say, but with Arianna conversation was easy, whether they spoke in Italian or whether Arianna practised her sometimes excellent, sometimes idiosyncratic English.

'Not annoying, working.' Arianna tilted her chin. 'This will all be mine one day; I need to learn how to look after it.'

She reminded Maddie so much of herself at a young age that her chest hurt with bittersweet nostalgia, old, weary scars flaring back to life. Once she had had the same pride in her name, in her surroundings, in her family. The difference being that Dante laughed at his daughter's arrogant words, swinging Arianna up in the air as he did so, whereas Maddie would have been hushed, reminded that the abbey would belong to her brother, not her. It seemed so harsh, to tell a child she was only a temporary resident, to ensure she never could feel fully at home. Harsh and useless, because Maddie had loved Stilling Abbey fiercely anyway. Part of her always would.

'Oh, well, in that case, I'm sure there are many jobs you can do, *cara*; I know the gardeners can do with someone to help them weed and the kitchen can always use another washer-upper. I did every job in this house at some point,' Dante added and Arianna stared at him solemnly.

'Then so will I.'

'Good girl, that's the best way to learn.' Maddie looked up at Dante, her heart squeezing at the sight of the tall man holding his daughter close. 'How's Luciana? Has her jet lag kicked in?'

'She's still in bed and if she doesn't get up soon it is going to take her whole stay before she adjusts. Ari, go and see if your aunt will wake up. I thought she might want to walk up to her favourite *ristorante* for lunch. The view's glorious,' Dante said to Maddie. 'You will love it.'

Maddie waited until Arianna had skipped out of the room before she replied. 'Do you think that's a good idea? If I accompany you on a family day out?'

'Of course.' He was completely the haughty aristocrat. 'Luciana was so weary yesterday she barely registered you. A family day out is exactly the kind of scenario she needs to see to stop her worrying.' He paused, the haughtiness slipping off his face. 'She looked so tired, even allowing for the jet lag and travel. I hope she isn't keeping anything from me.'

Maddie studied him, the worry in his eyes, etched into his face. On the drive back from Verona yesterday evening she had been struck by the easy, companionable bond between the siblings, evident despite the age gap, the distance that usually separated them. And she had been struck by the way they assessed each other when thought unseen. The concern shadowing Luciana as she glanced at her brother, mirrored by Dante whenever he looked back. For the first time she understood why Dante had lied, had wanted to stop the sister he evidently adored from fretting.

'It's a long journey; she's bound to be tired. The mountain air will do her the world of good.'

'So you'll join us?' It was more of a command than a request and, although Maddie still wasn't sure spending too much time in close proximity with Luciana was wise, she nodded her agreement.

'I realised yesterday that now you have agreed to pay for my ticket I can afford to leave at the end of the summer like I'd originally hoped. I'd like to be out of the country before Theo gets married, not because I think the press will chase me down or because I'll be broken-hearted, but because it feels right. Like the perfect time for a fresh start. It seems a shame not to see a little of the countryside before I leave and I still haven't explored the mountains at all.'

'Don't get carried away. This isn't a day out. You'll be working the whole time.'

'I know. Convincing Luciana we are in love whilst making sure Arianna suspects nothing.' Maddie slid out of her chair and stepped over to where Dante stood. 'Are you up to it, Conte?'

She didn't want to think about what she was doing, why her whole body was throbbing with desire as soon as she looked into his cool blue gaze, why her nerves were skittering in hope, in anticipation of his touch. They were planning a family walk, not an afternoon liaison. But all Maddie knew was that the moment Dante had dropped her off yesterday evening, she had been aware of just how alone she was for the first time since she had arrived in Italy. Her apartment no longer felt like a haven of independence, but small and cramped, her bed uncomfortable as she had tossed and turned, barely sleeping, reliving memories of the night before.

She wanted, needed more than memories. She needed touch. To touch and be touched. To be reminded that she lived. Existed.

What harm could a kiss do? Another night? Two or

three or four? She was leaving. So as long as she reminded herself that this was just an interlude before her
real adventures began then she was quite safe.

'You doubt my acting skills?' Dante's voice was
hoarse, his gaze no longer cool but full of heat, and
Maddie's whole body flamed at the sight, at the knowledge that she had elicited that reaction.

'No, I'm sure you'll be fine. But if you wanted a quick
rehearsal...' She allowed her voice to trail off suggestively.

Disappointment swept through her as he stepped
away, only to retreat as he slowly and deliberately, his
gaze holding hers, closed and locked the door to her office. 'A rehearsal sounds like an excellent idea, Signorina
Fitzroy. However, I can't promise it will be quick...' And
then, at last, his hands were on her as his mouth found
hers and Maddie kissed him back fiercely, slipping her
arms around him, luxuriating in the feel of his skin under
her fingertips. Surely she wasn't foolish enough to mistake this for anything more than lust and pleasure? No,
Maddie knew exactly what Dante was offering her, so
she might as well enjoy it while she could.

'Where have Arianna and Luciana gone?'

Dante looked up as Maddie rounded the corner, the
blood rushing to his veins at the sight of her. No cool,
professional Madeleine today. Instead her long, tanned
limbs were showcased by tiny denim shorts and her
close-fitting vest top, her silky hair pulled back into a
loose knot, tendrils curling in the heat. He liked seeing
the cool, organised Madeleine Fitzroy rumpled and casual. She looked very much as she had when he had left
her office earlier, rosy with exertion, damp with sweat.

He cast a quick glance around the mountain-top restaurant, cursing the other diners, the waiters, everyone
whose presence stopped him pushing her up against the
terrace balustrade and taking her right there, under the
mountain's gaze.

Dante swallowed, glad his voice remained steady.
'One of the other diners was driving back to San Tomo
and offered to give them a lift. It's a long walk back down
and they both seemed tired.'

'A lift sounds nice,' Maddie said. 'But I think I prefer walking down; it's all the extra pasta and bread and
tiramisu I have to carry with me I'm not sure about.
Why was I such a glutton? I must be at least a whole
other person heavier. In fact I don't need to walk; you
can probably just roll me down the mountainside.' She
joined him at the balustrade, leaning on it with a deep
sigh, one that seemed to come right from her toes. 'It is
so beautiful here. I know mountains, of course, but this
kind of Alpine lushness never seemed Italian to me before. Now it always will.'

Dante followed her gaze. The *ristorante* was high
on the mountain, right on a peak, with stunning views
across green valleys framed by white stone peaks. This
was his home, the landscape of his heart. And yet he had
exiled himself for five years, would spend most of the
year far to the south in the bustle of a city. Better not to
think about why, better to just enjoy every day as it came
and let the mountains and lakes restore his soul, a little
at a time. 'You ready to walk back?'

'I think so.' She patted her stomach. 'Let's take the
first part slowly though. I'm not joking about the rolling part.'

The paths were all clearly signposted, a vast network

of walks and hikes throughout the whole district. It was possible to take cable cars up to the next shelf, or down to the lower slopes, roads criss-crossed the mountains and valleys, but as they turned the corner and the *ristorante* was hidden from sight the modern world fell away. It was just the two of them in the majestic landscape. The path cut through a flower-strewn meadow populated only by mild, incurious cows, each adorned with a bell around its neck, the faint jingling adding to the birdsong piping up at intermittent intervals. Maddie didn't speak for the first few minutes, her eyes bright as she looked around her, her full mouth curved into a smile of pure joy.

'I could stay here for ever,' she said finally, so low he could hardly hear the words. 'Right here, right now. If there's a heaven then surely it must look like this. Oh, Dante. You are so lucky to belong here.'

But he didn't. Not any more. 'It's been too long since I've walked like this. Once I roamed these mountains more like a goatherd than a future *conte*, spent my winters skiing, the rest of the year climbing and walking. They were in my blood. Are in my blood. But Violetta didn't like to hike or to ski. She didn't like the mountains at all, said they were threatening, bleak. She saw beauty in restaurants and yachts, not in nature.'

'What a shame, to live surrounded by this and not to appreciate it.'

'The last two years of my marriage I would hike alone. Looking for answers, for peace, for happiness. But no matter how far I walked I could never leave my problems, my loneliness behind.'

The words just spilled out. Whether it was the way Maddie just listened quietly, no condemnation or surprise in her clear grey eyes, just acceptance, or whether it was the way they seemed alone in the world as they walked through the meadow, he didn't know.

'I'm sorry. There's nothing worse than a bad marriage. As someone who narrowly escaped one, I think I know what I'm talking about. Not that Theo isn't lovely—he really is. In a very driven, overactive way. But he isn't for me. And I'm not for him. We would have bored each other senseless within months.'

'By the end I would have settled for bored,' Dante said bleakly. 'Violetta liked to be the centre of attention. And for the first two years she was. But as time went by, as I recovered from my infatuation, the less time I had to spare to pander to her vanity. If I wasn't going to fawn over her, well, she would settle for an argument instead. It made no difference to her if I wanted to fight or not, or even if I joined in—she was quite capable of escalating up to full hysteria, complete with smashed ornaments and screaming, without my input.'

He stopped, shocked by how much he had revealed. He had never told anyone, not even Luciana, about the last eighteen months of his doomed marriage.

'Oh, Dante.'

'The more scenes she created the more excuses I found to stay away, to travel.' Dante rubbed his chin wearily, the rasp of his stubble grazing his palm. 'It was wrong of me. It just inflamed Violetta more and of course it meant I didn't see Arianna for days, sometimes weeks at a time. Violetta would accuse me of not caring about our daughter, she would say I resented her for being born, that I blamed her for our marriage. She would say it in front of her—I don't know how much Arianna remembers. She was only three when Violetta died.'

'I can see why it was easier to stay away. For Arianna's sake as well as yours.'

'I knew she was safe.' Dante couldn't stop now. The words lancing his wounds. Painful as it was to excavate the ruins of his marriage like this, excruciating as it was to see with the clearness of hindsight just where he had gone wrong, it was still somehow cleansing, letting someone else hear the evidence and pronounce judgement. 'Violetta lost interest in her very early and left her to her nanny much of the time while she visited Milan and Rome. She hated San Tomo, complained that she was lonely, and I expect she was. None of her friends were there and she was a woman who needed the adulation, the stimulation of others to keep her happy. I should have agreed to her demands that we move to Milan, but I wanted my daughter raised in the *castello* as Luciana and I had been. And I didn't trust Violetta. Left to her own devices in a city for much of the time, I feared she would embarrass me. I was young. It's not an excuse, but I hadn't learned the art of compromise.'

'Some people never learn it. And you *were* young.'

They reached the pine forest and Dante led the way in, glad of the gloom, the trees towering overhead. 'At times I almost hated her.' He'd never said the truth aloud, barely even admitted it to himself. 'And I despised myself for being so weak because when she decided to turn on the charm in the beginning I fell, even knowing how temporary the reconciliation would be. Knowing she had as little respect for me as I had for myself, as I had for her. By the time I became immune to her charm we were locked in a self-destructive spiral, but I didn't want to admit to myself, to the world that I had made such a monumental mistake. Nor did I want to lose Arianna, and Violetta made it clear they came as a package. She might not want to be troubled with a child most of the time, but she didn't want me to have her either.'

'What happened?'

He exhaled, the memories toxic. 'Violetta had been away partying a lot and I put my foot down. Young and arrogant and embarrassed is a bad combination and I handled the situation—handled her—badly. I see now I should have let her go. Given her the house in Milan she demanded and let the marriage slowly disintegrate. The shine of the title had worn off by then; I don't think it would have taken much persuasion by a suitable lover for her to walk out. Instead I threatened to cut off her allowance if she didn't calm down, insisted she spend the winter at the *castello*. That she act like the Contessa Falcone, like a mother. And then I went away again, on a three-week business trip to the other side of the world, feeling as if I had acted like a man, solved the situation.'

'No one likes a tyrant,' Maddie said, but there was no condemnation in her voice. That was fine. Dante had enough for both of them.

'No. I didn't try and understand how Violetta felt. Didn't appreciate that she was highly strung and spoiled and bored. That she wanted the besotted boy who had danced attendance on her and told her that she was the most beautiful, desirable woman in the world, not a tired businessman who spent half of his life on planes and the other half in his study. Who didn't ever want to party unless there was a deal to be done, had no interest in her life, in her friends. Who treated her like a frivolous, naughty child, who reserved all his spare time for their daughter. You see...' he managed a smile but he knew it was bleak '...we were equally at fault. And so...she decided she had had enough. That she would leave me. In typical Violetta fashion she decided to do it as dramatically as possible. I know now she had several lovers during our marriage. She contacted the most recent and begged him to rescue her and he set off straight away.'

'Only they never made it. How sad.'

'They were both drunk and there was evidence of cocaine use. I had no idea she used, missed all the signs, although looking back it was clear she'd been using from the start. He drove too fast, skidded on some ice and the next moment Arianna was motherless and I a single parent.'

'I am so sorry.' Maddie slipped her hand into his, clasping him tightly. Her hand felt so comfortable, so right. He clung on with no idea how to let go.

The fact he didn't want to let go was the most terrifying thing of all.

'I made a vow that day that Arianna would never suffer for my mistakes. That I would always put her first, be father and mother to her. And I also vowed that I would never be so foolish again, never let lust blind me. You want romance, Maddie? You're not alone. Oh, those people looking at that balcony yesterday, like you, they believe in love, in fate and destiny. But love blinds you, makes you act like a fool. It's not beautiful or perfect, it's cruel and demanding. It's capricious, temporary. Be careful it doesn't hurt you. You might decide your Earl wasn't such a bad bet after all.'

Maddie halted and turned to him, her eyes full of compassion. 'She really did a number on you, didn't she?' she said, her mouth quivering. 'It's absolutely fine to learn from our mistakes, Dante, but we shouldn't dwell on them. And learning means we do better next time.

Don't shut yourself off because of one bad experience. You have a lot to offer the right woman. A lot beyond the castle and the title and the rest.' She stood on her tiptoes and pressed one light, sweet kiss onto his mouth. He wanted to grab her, consume her, but stood motionless as she pulled away.

Because she was wrong. He had nothing to offer beyond the castle and the title. The rest had been buried with his wife—and it was no more than he deserved.

CHAPTER NINE

'DANTE SEEMS VERY taken with you.' Luciana slid a sly smile Maddie's way. 'A sister can tell these things.'

'Oh, no,' Maddie protested. 'It's still just…'

'Still just early days. I know. He keeps telling me the same—as if that will change anything. Just like he thinks he's doing his best not to look at you when other people can see. But he can't help it. He thinks I don't notice but I do.'

Maddie hid a wince. Luciana was noticing things that definitely weren't there. Things had been decidedly cool between Dante and Maddie over the last week. It was as if he had shown her too much on the walk through the mountains and it had spooked him—which was probably for the best. Maddie could manage the haughty Conte, could just about handle the passionate man who made her body tremble—but Dante opening his heart, show-ing her his vulnerabilities was too much for her. She wanted to make things better, to heal him, to show him that love didn't have to hurt.

Which was ironic, because seriously, what did she know about love? Besides, Dante was exactly the kind of man she had sworn to steer clear of: rich, titled, owner of the kind of ancient house she could manage in her sleep.

She was bred to wed a man like Dante and the whole reason she had left England was to forge her own destiny, not revert to type.

'What a beautiful day.' Luciana stretched luxuriously. 'I could lie here for ever.' It was a perfect day, with the sun delivering exactly the right degree of heat, the light illuminating the mountains and the water so they almost hurt with their intensity and vibrant colour. Maddie and Luciana had brought Arianna down to the small lakeside beach and were lying on sunbeds, toasting themselves, while she splashed around in the shallows with the insouciant resistance of youth to the chill of the water.

'Me too. I can't believe my next bride arrives tomorrow and my vacation is over.'

It had been an action-packed few days. They had explored more of Lake Garda, visiting several of the villages and towns along its banks, and spent another day trekking high into the mountains, before taking Arianna to a thrillingly long summer toboggan run. The night before, Dante had carried out his promise—or threat—to take them to the opera and, to her surprise, Maddie had found herself absorbed in the tale of passion and tragedy unfolding on the stage in front of her, swept away by the music and performance.

Luciana was sharp and funny, Arianna delightful. And Dante the consummate host. Everything would have been perfect if it weren't for the undercurrent of uncertainty that ran between Maddie and the Conte. That knowledge of something hot and powerful. If only she didn't know how his muscles felt under her questing fingertips, didn't know how his skin tasted. Didn't know the precise shade of blue his eyes darkened to when passion consumed him. She was on edge around him, every nerve attuned to his touch, jumping in response to a casual hand on her arm, her body reacting to the most polite smiles.

And Luciana watched it all. Of course, she thought they were hiding a real relationship from Arianna. She had no idea they were covering up a real temporary relationship from each other.

Luciana turned to look at Maddie, her expression hidden behind her oversized sunglasses. She was a formidably beautiful woman, tall and voluptuous with an air of complete certainty that everyone wanted to be near her, would indulge her. And they did. She was a universal favourite with all the castle staff, could coax Dante into anything. Maddie envied her poise, her appetite for life. 'Do you get much time off when there are weddings here?'

'Not much.' Maddie closed her eyes as she felt the sun soak straight into her bones. 'There are always other people on duty, of course, but I like to know what's going on at all times.'

'But your guests don't stay for the full week? The *castello* is back to normal two days a week?'

'They usually arrive on Friday afternoon and are gone by lunchtime on Wednesday,' Maddie confirmed. 'It gives us plenty of time to set up for the next family.'

'Hmm. That gives me an idea, but I need to speak to Dante. Talk of the devil. Dante, *cara*, over here.'

She waved and Maddie's heart jumped at the sight of the tall figure walking towards them. She suddenly felt exposed in nothing but her bikini, even though the sensible black design covered far more of her body than Luciana's flamboyant leopard-print confection.

'Ciao.' He stood in front of them so Maddie would

have to crane to look up at him. Instead she focused her gaze firmly out on the lake, watching Arianna practising her dives off the jetty. 'Luciana, I meant to ask. Do you want me to drive you to the train station tomorrow or are you hiring a car and driving to Lucerne? I'd lend you one of the *castello* four-wheel drives but you're flying back from Switzerland, aren't you?'

'In a hurry to be rid of me, *mi hermano*?'

'Not at all,' he said. Maddie could feel his gaze on her and could almost read his mind. When Luciana went they would no longer have any need to pretend, no reason to spend any time together. Relief mingled with regret. Maddie would ready herself to leave and Dante would sink back into the same solitary life he'd been determinedly not enjoying for the last five years. She brushed away the twinge of regret. That was his choice.

'But,' he continued, his gaze still burning into Maddie, 'I know you only have a week left and Mama is missing you too. It would be selfish of me to keep you from her.'

Luciana didn't answer for a few moments and when she did she didn't answer her brother directly. 'It's Mama's birthday in two weeks' time.'

'*Si*. I am planning for Arianna and myself to spend a couple of days in Lucerne and to take her out for lunch.'

'Lunch? For her sixtieth birthday? For shame, Dante.'

'As she won't admit to a day over fifty-four, I'm not sure it matters,' he said drily. 'What do you suggest instead?'

'A ball. Here, like the ones we used to have. Oh, Dante. It would be gorgeous and Mama would be so happy. What do you say?'

Maddie stopped pretending not to listen, turning to

Luciana in surprise as Dante exclaimed, 'A *what*? Impossible!'

'Why? Maddie has told me that there are no wedding guests staying here on a Wednesday or Thursday night. We could hold the ball on a Wednesday. Set up as soon as your wedding guests have gone. Oh, Dante, remember the balls Mama and Papa used to hold? The music and the dresses—flowers everywhere. So elegant. I couldn't wait for the day I could stop peeping through the gallery and actually attend myself...' Luciana stopped, lost in a nostalgic reverie and, despite herself, Maddie caught Dante's grimly amused eye. He grimaced at her before returning his attention to his sister.

'And when do you propose to hold this ball? Next week?'

'Don't be ridiculous. That doesn't give us nearly enough time. No, the week after.'

'The week after!' Maddie exclaimed as Dante said, 'You're serious?'

'Of course I'm serious.' Luciana sat up and removed her sunglasses, all the better to fix her brother with a hard stare. 'It's our mother's sixtieth birthday, Dante. She was still in mourning for her fiftieth. Remember? I persuaded her to come over to New Zealand, but her heart wasn't in it. Let's give her the kind of party Papa would have wanted her to have. I know it's short notice and I know it'll be a lot of work, but if we all work together I'm sure we can do it.'

'You won't even be here in two weeks!'

Luciana smiled up at her brother. 'I can change my flight. In fact, I spoke to Phil yesterday and he's going to see if he can get the school to let the boys have a couple of weeks off. It would be lovely to show them the place I grew up in.'

Maddie couldn't help but admire Luciana's almost arrogant confidence that events would pan out just the way she'd decided. 'So you'd stay here and not go to Lucerne?' Maddie held her breath as she waited for the answer. She had promised Dante a week—and that week was almost up. She didn't know if she could manage another fortnight. Especially while he was so cold and shuttered whenever they weren't with Luciana.

'How could I leave with so much to do? Mama will get the train across to us—or Dante could collect her.'

'You have got it all planned out.' But to Maddie's surprise, Dante didn't sound so horrified by the idea.

'I know it sounds impossible. But whatever strings you can't pull, Dante, Maddie can. She knows everyone. I knew this was possible yesterday morning when I waited with her in her office. She was charming florists and suppliers until they were promising far more than she asked for. Besides, we have a whole castle's worth of staff to help; the chefs will be delighted to have the opportunity to impress Mama's society friends and your business contacts. How long since the terraces have been used to entertain, huh?'

Maddie had always thought it a shame that the dramatic terraces with their views of the lake and gorgeous fountains and colourful flowerbeds weren't open to the wedding guests, not even for photos. Guido had told her that the insurance was too prohibitive but she suspected it was more that Dante wanted to keep part of the *castello* private. She turned and stared over at the Castello Falcone with narrowed eyes, imagining lanterns lighting the steps, little tables and chairs set out on the lawns, a marquee down here by the lakeside… String quartets on the terraces, something more bluesy here and a proper dance band in the Medieval Hall. 'But who would come on such short notice?' she asked, reality reasserting its prosaic head.

To her surprise the brother and sister looked at her with identically amused—and slightly smug—expressions.

'The first party at the Castello Falcone in over a decade?'

'The problem will be stopping gatecrashers, not getting people to come.'

'Many of Mama's friends spend the summer in the lakes and mountains anyway. No one is an impossible distance away. And those who are further away or abroad? I'm sure there will be some quickly cancelled plans,' Luciana said. 'There are plenty of unused bedrooms; we can easily put up the aunts, uncles and godparents in the *castello* itself. Run coaches down to Riva for everyone else.'

Dante stared across the lake, brow furrowed in thought. 'I agree it's a lovely thought, Ciana, and Mama would love it, but…'

'Then it's decided!' Luciana jumped to her feet with the litheness of a girl of sixteen rather than a thirty-something mother of three. 'Thank you, Dante! I'll call Mama right now and get the guest list settled and find out when she wants to come and then I'll call Phil and tell him to get booking flights. I can't wait for Arianna to meet her cousins. Ari,' she called over to the still-swimming child. 'Come back with me? I'm going to call your *nonna* and then you and I need to plan a shopping trip to Milan!'

Arianna shouted back her agreement, emerging from

the water like an enthusiastic Labrador, shaking water everywhere without a care as she grabbed her flip-flops, bestowed a quick soggy hug on Maddie and her father and ran after her aunt. Dante stood stock-still, staring after his sister, before shaking his head and barking out a short, humourless laugh. 'I should have known she didn't need me to actually consent. As soon as she thought of it, the ball was a done deal.'

'At least Arianna will be happy her aunt's staying longer,' Maddie said cautiously, horribly conscious that this was the first time she and Dante had been alone in the week since they'd returned from their mountain walk. She didn't want to look at him but her gaze was inexorably drawn to his. He looked tired, stubble on his usually clean-shaven jaw. Had the last week been as much of a burden for him as it had been for her?

'She's had a wonderful week. She adores Luciana—and she's really taken to you. It's going to be hard on her when her aunt returns home and you leave. I think we'll return to Roma then; it'll be easier for her to adjust back in the city. Look, this plan of Luciana's; she's obviously expecting you to help. It's not part of your duties. I'll talk to her.'

'No, honestly, Dante, it's fine. I don't mind.'

His brows rose. 'You don't mind suddenly having to organise a ball for what, I will warn you, will probably be two hundred people in just over ten days?'

'Not at all. It's not like I'll be doing it all alone and Luciana's right—we have a lot of expertise here in the castle. Besides, she's counting on my help. I don't want to let her down.'

'Did she ask you to help?'

'Not exactly. I've only just heard about it as well. But I would have said yes anyway. I like to be useful.'

'Tell me, Madeleine Fitzroy. Do you ever say no or are you so desperate to be needed that you'll say yes to anything that comes your way? Seven-day weeks? Impromptu balls? Marriage to a man you don't love? A fake relationship? Did I even need to agree to financial inducement or would you have agreed anyway? Always accommodating everyone but yourself.'

Maddie froze at the mockery in Dante's voice. She'd thought—what? That maybe he liked her just a little too much; that was why he'd kept his distance from her. Stupid girl. He thought her a doormat, nothing more. And he was right.

She clambered to her feet with a tenth of the lithe grace Luciana had displayed, hurt making her limbs clumsy as she grabbed her sundress, wrapping it around her body as if it were armour, securing the belt with unnecessary vigour. 'I'm saying no to this conversation.' Proud of how strong her voice sounded, she stuffed her feet into her sandals and took off, away from the *castello* and duty and a family she was once again on the outside of. She didn't much care where she walked. She just needed to get away.

'Damn.' Dante cursed as he watched Maddie march away, tall and elegant—and hurt. Hurt he had caused with hateful words. Words designed to provoke a reaction. Any reaction. Which made him no better than Violetta...

Maddie had been so hard to read all week. Friendly with Luciana. Sweet with Arianna. Courteous and polite to him, no less, no more. She'd fulfilled their brief perfectly. Luciana was sure they were mad for each other, was urging him to make it public. 'Only people hot for each other are so very cool,' she had told him gleefully.

But Maddie had been very careful not to catch his eye, not to be alone with him. Her hand hadn't sought his, her smiles were for others. There had been no intimacy, verbal or otherwise, since they had walked back from the mountain. Since he had opened his heart to her.

But, he hadn't reached out either. Hadn't wanted to overstep, take her generosity for granted. Had he—maybe—come over as a little stand-offish? Violetta's angry words rang in his head, as clear and potent now as they were five years ago: *'You are a statue, Dante. Carved out of nothing but marble. No emotion, no fire. I need a real man.'*

Was that what Maddie had seen this last week? A statue? Had he used up all his openness as they walked down the mountain before retreating behind his mask? Dante suspected the answer might be yes. Even last night, at the opera, he had confined himself to commonplace remarks about the music and plot, been assiduous in providing refreshments and making sure Maddie and Luciana were comfortable, but he had barely even told Maddie how beautiful she was—and she had looked spectacular in a dark blue jumpsuit, her hair twisted into a loose braid. Nor had the music swept him away as it usually did. He'd been too on edge, distracted.

'Accidenti,' he cursed again and then, before he could remind himself why keeping his distance was a good thing, he took off after Maddie, jogging along the river path.

It didn't take long to catch her up; she was standing by

the lake just a few hundred metres along the path, staring into its blue depths, her expression as inscrutable as ever.

'*Mi perdoni*. I was very rude. It was inexcusable.'

Maddie didn't answer for a long moment. When she did her voice was bleak. 'Yes. You were. But it doesn't mean you weren't right.'

'I have no right to judge you; I barely know you.'

She flinched at his words. 'No. I don't suppose you do. I don't suppose anyone does. Not even me. That is what this time away from England is supposed to be— trying to find out who I am when I strip away family and strip away obligation. But all I did was get caught up in your family dramas.'

'I asked you to.'

'And I jumped at the chance. You're right, Dante. I need to be needed. I want to be wanted. If I'm not useful, then who am I?'

'Maddie, you are a warm, compassionate woman. A warm, compassionate, hardworking and intelligent woman. You don't need other people's approval to validate you.'

She looked up at him, her eyes so dark a grey they were almost black. 'I shouldn't but I do. Pathetic, I know. That's the worst part—I do know and yet I make the same mistakes over and over.'

'Maddie.' Dante stepped forward and laid a hand on her shoulder, her skin impossibly smooth, impossibly silky, and his hands ached with the memory of how soft she had been under his hands. How warm, how welcoming, how comforting. How intoxicating. 'I need to apologise for this last week. I put you in a very difficult position and I want you to know how much I appreciate it. It was always going to be hard lying to Luciana without adding in other complications...'

'By complications you mean sleeping together? That was my decision, Dante, and I own it. Let me have that at least.'

'But I allowed our intimacy to scare me away and that was wrong.'

'You've been avoiding me.'

'I have,' he confirmed. A wry smile escaped him. 'Which, considering I was simultaneously paying you to pretend to be my girlfriend, was foolish as well as rude.'

A brittle laugh escaped her. 'All you've done is convince Luciana that we are mad for each other. She's noticed how we never touch or look at each other and she's decided it's because we'd spontaneously combust if we did.'

'She might be right,' he said hoarsely. Satisfaction ran through him as Maddie quivered under his hand. 'Every time I look at you I remember what you feel like, what you taste like...'

'Please. Don't. It's hard enough.'

He stepped back, his hand dropping to his side, his whole body chilled despite the heat of the summer's day. 'I should never have asked you to lie for me. I just wanted...' He closed his eyes briefly, trying to find the right words. 'Sometimes, Maddie, it seems that all I do is hurt people—Violetta, Luciana, you—and yet all I want is to do what's right. I know that anything grounded in deceit is wrong and yet I blundered on and here we are. I should have been honest with Luciana in the beginning. Maybe it's time she and I have that conversation.'

Maddie frowned. 'I can't disagree; I think a lot of heartbreak could have been saved if you had been honest earlier. And maybe it is time to have a real, proper talk with your sister. But I also think you should wait until after the ball. Enjoy the next few weeks; save the serious discussion for afterwards. She looks so much better than when she arrived; wait till she's even more rested.'

'I can't ask you to keep pretending…'

'Yes. You can. You can ask—and then it's up to me to decide whether I am happy to carry on or not. But, Dante, if I do say yes there will be some rules. I may be your employee but that doesn't mean I don't deserve to be treated with respect.'

'Understood. I should never have made you feel that was in doubt.'

'No. And I shouldn't have allowed you to. Deal?' She held out her hand and Dante took it.

The feeling of coming home as he clasped her cool hand, felt her fingers enclose his, was so profound it almost hurt. Hurriedly he let go. 'Deal.'

'Okay. I'd better go. I have a feeling Luciana will have already stirred the entire staff up into a frenzy and we do have two weddings to host before the ball.' But although she shifted as she spoke she didn't actually move, her storm-coloured eyes fixed on his.

'This might be your last moment of calm for two weeks. If I were you I would enjoy it. I have a feeling everyone is going to be turning to you a lot over the next few days.' He hesitated. 'Maddie. You can tell me to go to hell but I have to ask. Why do you need other people's validation? You're clever and organised and brilliant with people. You're creative, clear-thinking—Guido has been singing your praises for months. The *castello* is actually beginning to pay its way and a lot of the credit for that goes to you. And, not that it should matter, but I have to be honest and point out that you are also incredibly beautiful and sexy as hell. The world should be at your feet. I see that, we all see that. Why don't you?'

Maddie just stood and stared at him, her mouth half-open in surprise. 'I… No one has ever said that to me before. Thank you.'

'Then you are surrounding yourself with the wrong people.'

'That is probably true. The problem is, I'm related to half of them.' She smiled but it was a half-hearted attempt.

'Didn't you single-handedly turn around your family fortunes?'

'Pretty much.'

'I'll love Arianna no matter what she chooses to do, but if she shows a tenth of the initiative and drive you did when she's sixteen I'll be unbearably proud. How can they not be?'

Maddie's smile didn't reach her eyes. 'The problem was, I was born first. That meant my parents had a couple of years of worry until my brother came along and made sure the title and estate were safely secured. You understand that; you have the Castello Falcone. It's bred into you. Part of you. Everything the whole family does is about preserving it, readying it for future generations. That's implicit. But if, like me, you're not destined to inherit, then you spend your whole childhood knowing you have to leave it. That you're only ever a visitor, a footnote in the family history, not the main character.'

She sighed and then began to walk along the path again away from the *castello*, Dante falling into step beside her as they rounded a bend and began to climb away from the lake and through the pine forest. After a long pause she began to speak again, almost as if she were speaking to herself. He just a bystander. 'It didn't make sense when I was little. I was the oldest—not that being the oldest necessarily makes anyone the perfect heir, but still—so why was Teddy going to inherit? I just couldn't understand it. But every time I pointed out how unfair it was for women to be excluded from the succession it was as if I was committing family treason—it was even worse when I got briefly involved with a pressure group of other women pushing for change in the archaic laws.'

'Did your family feel as if you were criticising them?'

'Maybe. I didn't mean any of it personally, but of course my father had an older sister; his father too. I can see why they were—are—so resistant.' She sighed. 'They weren't even that comfortable with all the work I did to make Stilling Abbey profitable—because the money goes with the title. It wasn't really my place to get involved. I just didn't *know* my place, that was the problem—is the problem. Now I don't know where I belong at all. That's what I need to figure out.'

'You must have been lonely.' Dante couldn't imagine it. He too had been brought up in a grand old house owned by generations of his forebears, although he knew, unlike Maddie, that one day it would pass to him to look after. But, although he and Luciana had been brought up in a house that was larger than the norm, older than the norm, it was still filled with love and affection.

'I was. You know, Teddy's school reports were exclaimed over, mine ignored, even though my marks were better. My mother wanted to know why I wasn't making the right friends, going to the right parties—fitting in and making social contacts were more important to her than any grade. My dad praised me when I looked nice, or if I was in some stupid catwalk show, or won a gymkhana, but he didn't ever praise my maths grades. I just wanted them to be proud of me. Is that so wrong?'

'It's not wrong at all.'

'They gave me my head for a time, but when Teddy finished university it was made clear that I had got too close. That I needed to step back, step away. Oh, they never said anything outright, but they froze me out.' Her voice broke and instinctively Dante reached for her hand and she grasped it as if he were a lifeline. 'That's when I went on a visit to Theo's parents' and I just never left. They needed me and they were so grateful for the smallest thing. It was intoxicating. I just wanted to be part of them, their family, their home. To be wanted and needed and appreciated. Marrying Theo would give me all that—a family. Only he didn't want or need me at all.'

'Then he's a fool.'

'No. He's not, although it's very kind of you to say so.'

'Maddie.' Dante halted, pulling her to a stop, and she looked up at him, her eyes still darkened to stormy grey. All he wanted was to wipe away the doubt and sadness he saw there. 'I can tell you honestly that everyone at the *castello* will miss you when you leave. And not just because you are hardworking, but also because you're you. When Guido heard you were leaving at the end of August he threatened to walk out unless I paid you enough to make you stay.'

Maddie's smile was tremulous. 'That's very kind of him.'

'Nonsense. No one cares about your name or family here. They care about you.'

Her smile was tremulous. Dante couldn't tear his gaze away from her full mouth, wanting to kiss the doubt and unhappiness away.

'I don't mind helping with the ball because I think it will be fun to see the *castello* in its full glory. And personally I would feel uncomfortable if Luciana knew we'd deceived her. I like her and I don't want things to be awkward. So I'd rather keep pretending until the ball is over if that's okay with you—I leave a few days later anyway.'

'Your ticket's booked?' Dante didn't want to think about why that thought disturbed him.

'I did it yesterday. Thank you. And for the bonus. It was more than I was expecting.'

'Enough for the sloths?'

'Oh, yes. I'm planning a whole week hanging out near the sloth sanctuary before I head down to Peru for trekking and culture. With the bonus and my savings I've enough to travel through Central America; I won't need to look for work until I get to Australia. So, do you agree? That it's best we keep pretending?'

Dante swallowed. 'I think that will work. I do have a suggestion though.'

'What's that?'

'Back on the boat, in Verona, we said we'd see how things went. Remember? I think we—I—have made a mess of this week. I'd like to do better.'

'Oh?' Maddie's mouth trembled. 'And how are you proposing to do that?'

'I was hoping...' He stepped forward, deliberately backing her up until she was leaning against a tree, her eyes shadowed by long lashes as he looked down at her. 'I was hoping we could seal our new start with a kiss.'

He waited, unsure whether he had overstepped, whether it was too late, whether reigniting the passion that had flamed so brightly it had almost burned him was a mistake. But all he knew was that he couldn't spend two more weeks with Maddie and not kiss her. Not touch her. Not consume her as she consumed him.

'A kiss? Is that wise?'

'Are kisses meant to be wise?'

'Maybe not,' she said and looked up at him at last, her eyes vulnerable in their trust, with their need. 'Maybe that's the point. Maybe that's what we both need, some carefree kisses.'

'Maybe.' But there was nothing carefree about kissing Maddie as his hand travelled down her arm to her waist, as his other hand tilted her chin, as his skin thrilled to her touch and his heart beat in unison with hers. As their eyes locked, as his mouth slanted towards her, as he heard her sigh in anticipation and his whole body thrilled in response he knew that every kiss would have its price. But there was no way he was going to stop. Could stop. Not while her touch urged him on, her body melding into his. Whatever the price, he was willing to pay.

CHAPTER TEN

'OH, MADDIE! THIS is wonderful. You are a genius.'

'I'm not sure about that,' Maddie said, laughing at Luciana's exuberance. 'Although the *castello* does look rather magical. But I had a lot of help. Everyone has worked so hard.'

They had. Not only the *castello* staff, who had pulled double shifts and forgone days off, but most of the village had turned out as well, offering their services as waiters, cleaners, pot-washers—anything that needed doing to ensure the ball was a success. Apparently it was a tradition for the villagers to help out at *castello* events, not just because they were well-paid for doing so, but also because the staff party that followed on was legendary and no one wanted to miss out. It was a little odd to see the schoolteacher mixing cocktails and the woman who cut Maddie's hair serving canapés, but it also made the whole ball feel even more like a family affair with everyone pitching in.

Luciana had insisted that Maddie should attend, despite her protestations that it was much easier to deal with any last-minute hiccups if she wasn't in a long dress and heels. But she'd been overruled. Maddie suspected that her friend just wanted to watch Dante and Maddie dance together. It looked as if Luciana would get her wish. Maddie had promised him one dance.

Just the one. Because tomorrow Luciana and her family would be departing back to New Zealand and there would be no reason for Maddie and Dante to pretend they were anything other than two lonely people who had made a temporary connection any more. This Cinderella would be jumping on a plane in just a few days and the Conte would return to Rome and his life there. It was time for their summer idyll to come to an end.

Which was all for the best because the last two weeks had been terrifying—a pretend girlfriend by day and a secret lover by night. The days had been easy. As predicted, she'd been far too busy to spend much time with Luciana and her family. The few moments she had been able to snatch away from her work she'd been busy booking accommodation in the US and Central America, making sure as much of her first month was organised as possible.

But at night…that was Dante's time and he made the most of it. Maddie was existing on barely any sleep and yet she'd never felt more energised. She finally understood why her friends had glowed at the beginning of a relationship, the potent, heady mixture of hormones and sex and desire making every nerve end come alive.

If only it were just sex. *That* she could handle. After all, she was well overdue an indulgent affair. But it was so much more—and that she was finding a lot more difficult to manage.

It wasn't that Maddie didn't appreciate the late-night lakeside picnics—and the late-night skinny-dipping. Or the evening trips back to Lake Garda for dinner on board the boat as it sailed out across the lake. Or the dinner in the tiny mountaintop restaurant. Or even the night he had brought pizza to her apartment and they'd eaten it in bed whilst he'd helped her plan out her first month's travels. No, she appreciated every moment of it. Only, in a way, she had preferred the morose man who couldn't even look at her.

Because that man would have been easy to leave.

Unlike the man whose smile still hit her with its sweetness, the man with the knowing touch, the sweet kisses and who seemed to know exactly what she wanted before she did.

She knew the rules. No strings, no ties, for a few weeks only. She'd helped write them after all.

She just hadn't appreciated how easy they would be to break.

'You look beautiful.' Arianna appeared at her side and was gazing up at Maddie with a worshipful expression that caught at Maddie's heart.

'So do you,' she said honestly. The usually grubby urchin who lived her life in shorts and a T-shirt was wearing a red dress, her dark hair shining as it fell down her back confined with a large bow.

Arianna pulled a face. 'Zia Luciana insisted. I would have refused, but she's made the boys wear suits.' She pointed over to the other side of the medieval hall where three small boys were standing scowling mutinously, each of them spic and span in neat blue suits. 'That's far worse, isn't it?'

'My sons look very handsome,' Luciana said indignantly. 'Come on, Arianna. Let's make sure your *nonna* is ready for her grand entrance. She wants all her grandchildren to escort her.'

'And then we can play!' Arianna twirled round, her

skirts swirling around her knees. 'Maddie, will you dance with me later? The boys don't dance. They think they are too cool.'

'No one is too cool to dance, don't worry, Arianna. I bet we can get those boys on the dance floor and having fun.'

'Run over to your cousins, Ari.' Luciana ran a hand through her small niece's hair. 'And take them up to Nonna's room. I'll be there in a minute. I just need to check everything is in place.'

'Luciana,' Maddie said, laughing as she watched Arianna strut over to her cousins, every step proclaiming that she was in charge. 'Everything is in place. We've been through it ten times.'

'The band know the signal?'

'Yes.'

'The guests all know to be in the hall?'

'I have people rounding up any strays.'

'Dante has his speech ready?'

'He was pacing up and down and muttering it to himself, so, yes, I believe so. Go, get your mother and we can get this party started.'

'You are an absolute treasure. There is no way I could have done this without you.'

'Nonsense!'

'I am serious. And my brother looks happier that I have seen him in a long time. Forgive me for saying this, but it's a different happiness to before. More measured, less feverish. He was a boy then. This is a man's happiness.'

'Luciana...' Maddie shifted, uncomfortable with the topic.

'And Ari adores you. My heart used to break for her,

but I can go back to New Zealand happy, knowing that you are here.' Luciana leaned forward and embraced Maddie with a kiss on both cheeks, before turning and heading out of the hall. Maddie stood and watched her go, her chest tight.

Everything had escalated so far beyond her control. She had never intended to get so close to Luciana—to like her, to enjoy her company. Now what had seemed like a harmless deception done for the best of intentions seemed cruel, manipulative. And as for Arianna... Maddie's chest tightened even more, the pain almost making her gasp. The one consolation was that the small girl didn't know about either the fake or the real relationship between her father and Maddie. But Maddie had allowed herself to get too close to the child. Had allowed herself to care for her—and, worse, she knew Arianna was getting far too attached, searching her out, confiding secrets, seeking reassurance.

At that moment she saw Dante. He looked good in formal evening wear, the severe, clean lines suiting his austere handsomeness. He stood, unsmiling, listening courteously to the elderly couple who had greeted him. Maddie watched him, drinking in every fibre of him. The dark hair she loved to muss out of its usual order, dark blue eyes capable of freezing—or heating—with one glance, sharp cheekbones, wide shoulders tapering down to a narrow waist. It may have been the way Dante looked that had pulled her in that first day by the lake; it was partly the way he looked that had enticed her to throw caution to the wind and stay with him on the boat that first time. But the pulse beating insistently at her neck, her wrists, the tops of her thighs had nothing to do with mere looks.

No. She was attracted to his quiet, un-showy thought-fulness. The way he wanted his sister to stop worrying, his dedication to his daughter, his commitment to the village and the people who worked at the *castello*. She was attracted to those rare flashes of humour. To the way his smile transformed his usual serious demeanour, giving him a warmth and sweetness most people never suspected that the Conte Falcone possessed.

And in just four days she would get on a plane and would travel to the other side of the world. It was unlikely she would ever see him again. Maybe that was for the best. Because whatever Dante wanted from the rest of his life it didn't include her.

As if he could hear her thoughts across the crowded room Dante looked over at her and their gazes caught for one long moment. Humour and heat mingled in his gaze and Maddie wished that she could walk over to him, slip her arm through his and claim him as hers, publicly and irrevocably.

Hang on. She *what*?

Taking a step back, Maddie was relieved to feel the cold security of the wall propping her up as her legs trembled, her stomach swooping like a starling in full murmuration. This wasn't the deal—not the deal she had made with Dante, or the one she had made with herself. The last few weeks had been the first step in a new adventure, in claiming her identity as a new Maddie. They hadn't been about putting down roots in any way, especially not romantically.

And yet that was exactly what she had done.

Somehow she had allowed Dante Falcone to claim a place in her heart—only, ironically, he had as little interest in being there as she had in having him there.

'Fool,' Maddie muttered. 'Utter fool.' Only she could get herself into this kind of mess. At least her departure date was fixed. If she could just make sure Dante suspected nothing, left with her head high and a smile on her lips, then at least her dignity would be intact. Just not her heart.

Dante took a breath, relieved to have a moment to himself for the first time that evening. It seemed that no time at all had passed since the Dowager Contessa had, as planned, descended into the medieval hall from the gallery above, flanked by her four grandchildren. She had been greeted by a room full of her friends and relatives, a large contingent of Luciana's friends and some of Dante's business associates, as well as family associates and neighbours. The band had immediately struck up a medley of her favourite songs, starting with the Beatles, before Dante had welcomed everyone to the first Falcone ball in over a decade and toasted his mother's health.

After the formalities the crowd dispersed. Some stayed in the hall to dance to a selection of sixties tunes, others mingled on the terraces or made their way to the marquee by the lakeside. Waiting staff circulated with trays of drinks and canapés, buffet tables were set up in the formal dining room and in the courtyard, and entertainers amused the partygoers with magic tricks, acrobatics and spectacular professional dancing. All the fountains had been switched on, water cascading down the series of terraces like a waterfall, illuminated by the lamps which had been threaded through all the trees and hedges. The Castello Falcone looked stunning, like a scene from a modern-day fairy tale. The last time it had been so vibrant, so alive had been for Dante's wedding.

Dante's mouth tightened. Violetta had been so excited she was getting married in a real castle—and he had been so proud that he could give her that opportunity. He had so willingly and happily bestowed his home, his title, his love on her. But all she wanted was the first two of the trio and even they had palled after a while. His love had never been enough.

It was funny that Maddie had almost married for the same reasons. That she too had chosen a title and a grand old house over love. Only in the end she had walked away.

He glanced at his watch. Half-past eleven. Half an hour until their dance. He had barely seen Maddie all night. She was supposed to be enjoying the ball as a guest, but she was probably running around behind the scenes, making sure everything was going smoothly. The only way to get her to stop would be to make her—he'd have to insist on a glass of Prosecco, maybe a walk down to the lake. Not that they would get any privacy with over two hundred guests plus staff milling around—and his mother, whose sharp, blue-eyed gaze missed nothing.

Maddie and he had managed to keep their liaison a secret from her so far; there was no point being outed now when his family were departing tomorrow and Maddie herself had booked her flight to leave in just four days' time.

Dante's hands tightened on his glass stem. He'd only known her for a few weeks and yet somehow she had become an integral part of his family, his life. Somehow Dante knew that the way she relaxed with him was unusual, a privilege. Not just in bed, but also the way she teased him, allowed him to tease her. The way she confided her hopes and dreams, her fears. Inspired him to confide his. Not many people saw that side of Maddie.

Maybe it was a good thing she was leaving before he got too used to having her around.

'Dante, there you are.'

He turned as Luciana called his name and smiled affectionately at his sister, magnificent in tight red silk. 'I have to admit I thought you were crazy when you suggested holding a ball in such a short period of time, but you have done a wonderful job. Mama looks radiant. She has barely left the dance floor all night.'

'Last I heard she was dropping all kinds of heavy hints about the years she spent in London before she married Papa. If we believe her then she was serially dating a number of rock 'n' roll stars! If I have to hear one more story about what she got up to in her "garret on the King's Road" then I am sailing off to the other side of the lake, just me, a bottle of Prosecco and no more mental images of my mother in a teeny miniskirt flirting with half of London.'

'She was really beautiful though. She still is,' he added hurriedly, just in case his mother was behind him. 'But I would still rather not hear about the time she posed nude for a certain celebrity photographer.'

'No. Really no,' Luciana agreed, snagging two glasses of Prosecco from a passing waiter and handing one to him. 'Here, to us. The Falcones. Who really know how to throw a party.' She frowned, glass still held up to his. 'Maddie should be here. I wouldn't have been able to organise half of this without her. I only had responsibility for the guest list—which, let me tell you, was no mean feat; the great-aunts were a week's work alone—and she did the rest.'

'She's very capable.'

'She's more than that. I love her, Dante. She's exactly what you and Arianna need. No nonsense, organised, she understands our world, but has a lot of heart. Mind you don't let her slip away.'

Deceiving his sister for one week had been hard enough. But deceiving her for two more weeks, watching her get close to Maddie, seeing the happiness in her eyes whenever she caught sight of the two of them together...that was a whole other level of deceit and he had struggled to reconcile it with his own code of honour and responsibility.

'Ciana...' he began impulsively, but was interrupted by Arianna, flying over to him, her hair its usual tangle, her sandals long since discarded and smears of something that looked very much like a good half of the chocolate fountain down her dress.

'Papa. Papa.'

'Si, cucciola mia.'

'Did you know Maddie is leaving?'

'What?' Luciana turned to him, eyes wide in surprise.

'This was only always a temporary job for her, *cara*.' Dante took Arianna's hand. 'She has been saving up to travel the world. Doesn't that sound exciting?'

'But I like her! I don't want her to leave.'

'Ari, we're leaving too. In just a couple of days. Your aunt and cousins will go back to New Zealand and Nonna will go home to Lucerne and you and I have to go back to Roma for school and work. It's been a lovely summer, but even the best summers turn into autumn eventually.'

He did his best to keep his voice light and unconcerned despite the tears gathering in Arianna's eyes, the suspicion and disbelief in Luciana's gaze and the

heaviness in his heart. He didn't really want Maddie
to fly off to the other side of the world. He would have
been quite happy to keep their relationship going for a
little longer, to allow it to peter out naturally. But this
was what Maddie wanted, what she had been saving for,
planning for, what she needed. Not a lonely widower
whose heart was so locked away the chains were probably rusty with disuse.

'Ari,' he said again, coaxingly. 'This separation isn't
for ever. You and I and Nonna are going to spend Christmas in New Zealand with Zia Luciana and the cousins.
They live on a huge vineyard in the mountains. Best of
all it will be summer there. We can spend our Christmas
boating and swimming—won't that be fun?'

'But Maddie won't be coming with us?'

'No, she won't. Maddie has her own life to live, *bambina*. Her own adventures to have.' Adventures far from
here. Far from him.

'Can't you tell her not to go?'

'No. And I wouldn't if I could. She's looking forward
to it very much. So, even though it's hard, you need to
remember you're a Falcone and say *adieu* with a smile.'

Arianna's lip wobbled and she turned and fled into
the crowd without replying. With a sigh Dante straightened and turned to meet his sister's accusatory glance.

'She's leaving?'

'Ciana…'

'Don't you *Ciana* me! Why didn't you say anything?'

'Because I didn't want you to worry. Look, I like
Maddie. But I did tell you that our friendship is still in
very early days. Maddie has plans. Plans that don't, can't
include me, and I have a life incompatible with those

plans. We both knew that when we got closer and nothing has changed.'

'Dante Falcone, you are a fool.'

Dante blinked at the vehemence in his sister's voice.

'That girl might be the best thing to happen to you, to Arianna. And you're going to just let her walk away?'

'I'm not going to just let her do anything. Maddie is a grown woman.' And he knew all too well what happened when plans, needs didn't align—chaos and heartbreak.

'Have you said anything, asked her to stay?'

'No. No, I haven't. Because it wouldn't be fair.'

'Why not?'

This was why he had lied in the first place: Luciana was relentless. Dante's control snapped. 'Because I am not the kind of man Maddie needs.'

'No? You keep telling yourself that, *mio fratello*. But I think she is exactly what *you* need. And if you don't at least ask her to stay then you're an even bigger fool than I thought.' And with those closing remarks Luciana grabbed another glass of Prosecco and stalked away, leaving Dante staring after her.

This—this was why he couldn't be honest with his sister. She didn't understand. How could she? He was the Falcone heir. Responsible for hundreds—thousands—of jobs. He had to look after the family empire, the livelihoods of dependents, investors and staff. Custodian of the family name, title, holdings for the next generation. Failure wasn't an option. And yet he had failed spectacularly. Failed at marriage. At parenting. At love. It wasn't pride or fear or heartbreak that stopped him trying again. It was pragmatism. He couldn't be trusted to give his heart to someone who wanted it, who would value it. It made sense to keep it guarded.

Only, Arianna had so enjoyed the company of her aunt and Maddie. She needed a mother figure in her life, someone close by, not half the world away. He had always promised himself that he would put his daughter first. Maybe he should reconsider his decision to never remarry. He could look for someone safe. Someone who knew the rules, played the way he did. Someone he could trust. A partner, not a lover. The idea had been unthinkable just a few weeks ago, but Maddie had thawed him. Given him some of his self-respect back. He would always be grateful to her for that.

Lost in thought, he made his way back to the ballroom for the midnight dance, which would be followed by the presentation of the birthday cake. The ball wasn't due to end until the early hours for those with the stamina to keep going. The first coach would head back to Riva at one; the last wasn't due to depart until five, after coffee and pastries had been served to the final guests. Dante had no doubt that his mother would be the last one on the dance floor.

As he reached the double doors he sensed someone watching him and, looking up, he saw Maddie. She stood just inside the doors, a little paler than normal, but otherwise her usual composed self. He knew she had spent the whole evening flitting between the kitchen, the ballroom and the dining room, anticipating problems and solving them before they occurred, making sure every guest was comfortable and happy. But there was no sign of the hard work on her face. Her blonde, silky hair fell in a shining sheet. She wore silver, just as she had that first night on Lake Garda, this dress floor-length and full-skirted, the strapless bodice revealing a tantalising hint of cleavage. She wasn't wearing any jewellery, her make-up subtle, letting the dress take centre stage. But no dress, no matter how expensive, could outshine Maddie. Dante swallowed as he surveyed her from head to toe. The dip of her waist, the swell of her breasts, the long-lashed eyes. She was so beautiful, so elegant. Like a young queen surveying her kingdom.

And she was his.

The possessive thought came from nowhere. Shocking in its certainty. Dante's hand tightened compulsively on his wine glass. Pushing the thought, any thought away, he strode towards her, watching every tell-tale sign that his presence affected her. The way her eyes widened, the hitch in her breath. The pulse beating wildly in her exposed throat. The primal side of him roared its approval, pheromones flooding the air so thick and fast it was as if he could see them rising in a cloud to envelope them, separate them from the rest of the room.

She was his. Tonight at least. And then he had to let her go.

As he reached Maddie the band quietened and the band leader took to the microphone to announce the midnight dance. His mother, escorted by one of her many admirers, took to the centre of the dance floor and, watched by the hushed, appreciative crowd, waited for the first strains of her favourite song. Finally they came, the unmistakable sounds of the Beatles' 'Something', and slowly the pair began to waltz and Dante held his hand out to Maddie.

'My dance, I believe.'

Without a word she came to him, her arms slipping around his neck as he held her close. Bodies melding together as if they belonged, the music taking over as he guided her around the floor.

'Had a good night?' she asked after a while as the song blended into 'And I Love Her'. Dante tightened his grip.

'I didn't see you all evening. I thought you were supposed to be a guest, not running around working.'

Her eyes fell, but not before he saw the shadow in them. 'I had a lot to do. That reminds me, Dante. Ari heard me discussing my plans with Guido and I'm afraid she was upset.'

'I know, she came to see me.'

'I'm sorry. I meant to talk to her and tell her in person. But how could I explain it was a secret and her aunt couldn't know? I just didn't realise she would be so upset.'

'She cares about you. We all do,' he added and her cheeks flushed a delicate pink. 'Luciana was there when Arianna came to me. She knows you're leaving too.'

'I'm sorry.'

'No, don't be. They had to find out sometime.'

'Is Luciana very cross with me?'

'No. She's cross with me. She thinks I should persuade you to stay.'

'I see.'

The music slowed again and he pulled her in tight. She fitted him so perfectly, as if she was made for him and he for her. But life wasn't that neat. Lust faded, love wasn't infinite and hearts weren't wise. Maddie had dreams, and he couldn't, wouldn't stand in her way. He didn't want to ever see the same disappointment in her clear grey gaze that he had seen every day in Violetta's during the last two years of their marriage. Maddie may have changed his life, given him hope—but she didn't belong with him, whatever other people said, whatever he might want in the secret places in his heart.

He came to a decision. 'Maddie, I need to speak to you. Alone. There's something important I want to give you.'

Maddie came to an abrupt stop. They stood there, looking at each other as the rest of the dancers swirled around them.

'Tonight?'

'Now.' Something had to change, Dante knew that now and there was no point delaying any more. He couldn't follow his heart—but he could listen to his head. Before she could reply the band struck up the familiar strains of 'Happy Birthday' as the chef wheeled in an enormous and elaborate cake. Dante swore under his breath and Maddie stepped back.

'You need to be here for this.'

'*Si*. Meet me by the lake. In fifteen minutes?'

Her laugh was nervous. 'You're being very mysterious.'

'By the lake. I'll see you there.'

She opened her mouth as if to speak and then nodded. 'Okay. Fifteen minutes.'

Dante stood still and stared at her, drinking her in. Unable to stop himself, he reached out and ran one finger down her cheek, feeling the shiver that ran through her at his touch in his very core. Was he about to make the biggest mistake of his life? Setting his jaw, he stepped back, finding the right smile as he turned and greeted his mother, leading her towards the cake, and by the time he managed to look back Maddie had disappeared.

CHAPTER ELEVEN

IT WAS A good ten-minute walk through the vast old *castello* and down the gardens to the lake, but Maddie was barely aware of her route, or who she spoke to on the way down. The terraces were almost deserted, most of the guests back in the ballroom for the toasts and cake, and she could slip down the steps unaccosted. All she could see was the curious expression in Dante's eyes, a mixture of longing and regret.

The marquee by the lake was similarly empty, the jazz band taking a well-earned rest, the staff back up at the *castello* for the next half-hour. Maddie made her way to the bar and poured herself a glass of wine before curling up on one of the cushion-strewn benches which looked out over the lake, her heart hammering. What was so urgent Dante had to tell her tonight?

And why did she have the very clear feeling she wasn't going to like what she heard?

'Here.' She jumped at the rough voice as Dante passed her a glass of wine and with a start she realised hers was empty. It was the first thing she had drunk all night. She had wanted to stay alert and in control in case anything went wrong. 'The hall is emptying. I think quite a few people are headed here.'

'Then let's go.' Maddie allowed Dante to pull her to her feet and lead her out of the marquee and along the same path they had trodden just a couple of weeks ago, when she had unburdened her soul for the first and only time. 'Did your mother like her cake?'

'*Si*, she's loved the whole evening. Thank you for all that you've done.'

'There's no need to thank me. I'm just happy it all worked out.'

'It all worked out because of you.' Her treacherous heart warmed at the praise, reaching for it greedily. 'You are part of the *castello*. Everywhere I go people sing your praises; they love you. No one wants you to leave.'

Maddie swallowed, her throat burning with suppressed tears. She loved Castello Falcone and all who lived and worked within it too. Walking away was going to be the hardest thing she had ever done, even harder than calling off her wedding. But just like her wedding she had no choice but to leave. She'd got too close, too involved, and for all it felt like home she knew she didn't really belong here either. 'It's a very special place,' she managed somehow, proud of how steady her voice sounded.

'My family adore you, especially Arianna.'

What on earth was going on? Why had he pulled her away from the ball to tell her this? 'Your family are amazing—and Arianna is a real credit to you. You've done a fabulous job with her, Dante. I hope you know that.'

He didn't answer for a while, waiting until they reached a small cove. Maddie had arranged for seats to be put there in case any guests strayed this far down the path and Dante guided her towards them. Any faint hopes he'd simply lured her away to kiss her faded as he sat on the seat opposite, leaning back so that they weren't even within touching distance. Maddie sipped her wine and waited, the blood rushing in her ears.

'She is lonely,' he said eventually, his voice emotionless. 'She is too much alone and her cousins are so far away. Arianna needs a mother. I need a partner. Someone who can help me run the Falcone business interests. Someone who understands diplomacy, society, business.'

Maddie stilled as hope unfurled a tentative tendril. 'That makes sense.'

'I chose badly last time. Let my heart lead my head. I can't afford to do that again. Can't put my family, my daughter through that again. I always hoped that if I met someone I could trust, someone who understood my world then maybe I could contemplate marriage again, but I never thought it really possible. And then I met you.'

She watched him, the austere lines of his face softened by the moonlight and the lanterns strung around, and the realisation that had hit her in the ballroom returned in all its painful intensity. She loved him. Loved him in a defy-her-family-and-perish-in-a-tomb kind of way. Completely and utterly.

Earlier this evening she had vowed not to act on it, not to let him know. Was it possible she had got it all wrong? That there was a happy ending to the ball for her?

Say it, Dante, she begged him silently. *Tell me you love me.*

But he didn't look like a man on the verge of a declaration, more statue than flesh and blood, a muscle beating in his jaw the only sign that he felt anything at all. 'These last few weeks I've realised I can't let the past hold me back, can't let the past spoil my daughter's future. Maddie, you have shown me that companionship needn't be a war zone. That marrying again is probably the best thing I can do for my family, for my home.'

'Oh.' How was her voice so calm when inside she was more turbulent than a storm-tossed sea? Hope and joy and anger and disappointment and dull, dreary grief all jostling for prominence. Was this a proposal? A warning? A bid for her blessing? She couldn't tell. And she didn't know which of the answers was worse. What she did know was that a treacherous part of her was hoping that it *was* a proposal, blunt and prosaic as the words were. Not because of his title, not because of the *castello* or the fortune or any of the trappings that she had allowed to sway her before. But because she loved him.

Fool, she told herself fiercely. Someone threw her a few scraps, praised her and she was so grateful she just fell at their feet? Whatever Dante had just said to her, surely it couldn't be a proposal? Because if it was that then it would break her. Surely Dante knew that. He knew what she yearned for. Had made her feel that maybe it was possible. That one day someone would see through the cool, poised, organised façade and love the girl within. She'd known Theo a lifetime but he had never seen that need in her and she hadn't understood him in return. She'd only known Dante a month but already understood him all too well. Knew he was afraid. Afraid to feel. To love. The words he had just uttered a final proof, if one were needed.

Could she stay with him on that basis? Be part of this beautiful place? Help raise Arianna to become the exceptional young woman Maddie knew she could be? Marry the man she loved, knowing he would never be able to give her his heart, his soul? The part of Maddie who still felt she wasn't worthy of a heart and soul, who just needed to be needed, who just wanted a home, was shouting loudly that of course she could.

It was so tempting.

But not tempting enough.

Besides…he hadn't actually asked her.

The silence stretched out, long and uncomfortable, as Dante visibly searched for words. 'I'm not looking for love, Maddie. Love is an illusion. A drug. It passes and when it's gone it leaves nothing but hollowness and regret. Esteem, compatibility, respect? These are much better foundations to build a life together on.'

'Are they? I've been there, Dante, and I don't agree.'

'I know you walked away from such a marriage before, but this is different. I'm different.'

Yes. It was different. It was worse. Theo wasn't capable of breaking her heart, but the man next to her had infinite capacity to do so. And he was.

'You deserve better, more. Arianna deserves more.'

But it was as if he hadn't heard her. Instead he reached into his pocket. 'I have something for you.'

Time froze, the air still, the faint sounds from the ball receding away to little but echoes. What was he doing? Was this a ring? If there was a ring and a bended knee, would she be able to walk away? What if he said those three words she'd waited her whole life to hear? But the package he pulled out was too big to be a ring, a rectangular package. He held it out to her wordlessly and she took it in trembling hands, folding back the silk it was wrapped in.

A book.

'It's a travel journal. For you to capture your memories.' His eyes were on her, hunger and regret mingling in their blue depths. She turned the book over and over. It was handmade, illustrated, exquisite. It was almost the perfect present.

Almost...only it meant goodbye. This book was Dante's way of sending her away. He was going to marry someone else, some perfect stranger he would never love. 'It's beautiful.' Tears gathered in her eyes, hot and thick, spilling down her cheeks faster than she could wipe them. 'Thoughtful and...' She couldn't finish. 'Dante. Please. Don't marry someone you don't love.'

Carefully she wrapped the book back up and got to her feet, walking over to him and pulling him to his feet in turn. He didn't resist, but nor did he touch her in return. The book was a goodbye and he had already retreated from her.

'Don't marry someone you don't love,' she repeated. 'Not when we have this. It's rare and wonderful. Don't throw it away.'

She reached up and ran a hand along his jaw, searching his gaze as she did so. There was desire, yes. Heat. Resignation. And hope. Maddie knew, even if he hadn't admitted it to himself, that part of him was begging her to take a chance on him, to thaw him out, to hang on in there and hope that one day he would be capable of loving her.

But that wasn't enough. Maddie wanted someone who was capable of loving her now. Of needing her, not because of what she could do for them, but because of who she was.

'Don't give up on love,' she begged him and, standing on her tiptoes, she pressed her mouth to his.

He didn't stop her, didn't step away; instead he kissed her back, fiercely and hard. This was no sweet farewell or romantic goodbye; it was hard and unyielding and raw and Maddie took every moment of it, digging her hands into his hair, sliding them down his back, remembering every muscle and sinew in his glorious body, allowing him to explore her with the same fervency and need. It would be so easy to base a marriage on this. So very easy, and if she suggested she stay, she suggested he marry her, she thought he would probably agree.

Instead she stepped away, instantly cold as she stood alone. 'I'd rather be alone my whole life than settle, Dante.'

'You won't need to. One day someone will come along who deserves you.'

'Maybe. But I need you to know,' she summoned up all the courage she had, 'I need you to know that if you had been able to tell me that you loved me tonight and asked me to stay then I would have said yes. That if you allowed yourself to love me I would stay. I'm not Violetta. And you're not the boy you were back then. We're two adults who could have made each other very happy, I think.'

She stepped closer again, allowing her body to thrill to the sensation of his nearness one last time as she pressed a final kiss to his cold cheek. 'Goodbye, Dante.'

And she turned and walked away.

The next few days passed in a merciful blur. Somehow Dante had managed to get back to the party, thrown himself into being the consummate host, the dutiful son, convincing everyone that he was having a fantastic time. But as he laughed and danced and entertained the remaining guests he was numb inside. It was as if his body had been taken over by someone who knew what to say, what to do, while Dante had shut down.

Maddie loved him.

And he had stood there and allowed her to walk away. What had he thought would happen? That she would listen to his plans for a sedate, sensible life and offer to be part of it? That wasn't what he wanted anyway. There was nothing sedate about Madeleine Fitzroy.

Besides, he knew who she was, what she wanted, and he would only have been able to offer her a pale facsimile of that. What had she said in Verona? 'If anyone ever proposes to me again I want romance and heart.' He had no romance and his heart was closed.

But if his heart was closed, then why were her words, her absence haunting him like this? If a business deal fell through then sure, it stung, but he didn't dwell on it. Learned any lessons needed and moved on. Didn't wallow in failure.

Dante sat back in his chair and allowed his glance to focus on the picture of Arianna framed above his desk. She looked so like her mother in that picture. The same mischievous expression, the same glossy hair and pointed chin. Only her eyes, a dark, long-lashed blue, came from him. And for once the resemblance to her mother didn't invoke the same old sickening guilt.

The truth was he had really, truly thought he was in love with Violetta. He'd been captivated by her. Infatuation, maybe, but it had felt more real at the time than anything he had ever experienced. He knew, then, just why Romeo had come hotfoot back to Verona, poison in hand, to die by the side of his love, because, then, the thought of life without Violetta had been unbearable. She had consumed him, subsumed him and he had fallen gratefully at her feet. Looking back, he could see why. It wasn't just her opulent beauty, her sensuality, her capricious sweetness—he had been lost, searching for a sense of who he was. His father's death had been so sudden, so unexpected, leaving Dante with responsibilities he hadn't expected to shoulder for another twenty years. Luciana was leaving Italy for good, and his mother, heartbroken, had retired to Lucerne, so she could build a life free of constant reminders of her beloved husband.

There Dante had been, just twenty-two, unsure of who he was, how he would cope, and Violetta had given him a path. He'd seen himself through her eyes—or so he thought—and a powerful, attractive man had stared back at him. He'd wanted to be that man so badly and, rather than grow into him, learn to be him, he'd taken a shortcut and allowed his relationship with Violetta to define him. Ironically, in the end, it had been the birth of Arianna which had both made him into the man he had wanted to be and signalled the end of his marriage. The moment he'd held his daughter everything made sense. She came first. For her he threw himself into work, building on his father's legacy, safeguarding and growing the Falcone business and investments. But as his life had fallen into place, as his way became clear, Violetta's had begun to fall apart. Without his besotted admiration she didn't know who *she* was, motherhood bored her and she had no interest in working beside him.

He saw it all so clearly now. But back then he had been at the mercy of his emotions, and they had led him badly astray, not just at the beginning, but also all the way through his marriage. He hadn't had the maturity or the common sense to handle his wife.

He wasn't responsible for her death. Only Violetta

had made the choice to get into that car, to take those drugs. But he carried responsibility for the death of his marriage. His love hadn't grown as he matured; rather it had withered away and he had blamed Violetta for that. To be fair to Violetta, she had always been true to herself; she hadn't changed. He had.

But what if Arianna had been in that car?

The thought still kept him awake at night, haunted him. He could have lost his daughter that day. She had to come first. And that meant ensuring he didn't allow his emotions to influence his decision-making. Not even—especially—where his relationships were concerned.

Arianna was hurting now. But she would understand one day that everything he did, he did for her. Wouldn't she?

He sure as hell hoped so. Because right now he was struggling to understand himself. That insistent feeling that maybe he was making the biggest mistake of his life. That he was holding himself back through fear. Through stubbornness.

Dante turned back to his computer, staring at the spreadsheet awaiting his comment as if it might have the answers, his mind unable to focus on the numbers.

He and Arianna had returned to Rome two days before and were installed back in the luxurious villa he had bought five years ago. It had been decorated and furnished by one of the city's top interior designers to fit his brief of a comfortable family home and yet somehow it never really *felt* like home. He'd always liked the Eternal City, but living there full-time, even with the benefit of extensive private gardens, was just too much. So much traffic, so much noise, so much hustling and busyness. A world away from the tranquillity of San Tomo and

Castello Falcone. He'd wanted that contrast then. Now every car horn, every shout, just reminded him of everything he didn't have.

He glanced at his watch. Noon. Maddie would be on her way to the airport, if she hadn't arrived there already. Her flight to New York left at three. She was spending three nights in the city before taking the train down the East Coast all the way to Florida, stopping at several destinations along the way, before flying down to Costa Rica and beginning her travels proper. He could see her, her travel bag on her back, hair scooped back into a no-nonsense ponytail, her eyes determined.

He knew every step of those first two weeks of her travels. From the moment she booked into the five-star hotel in New York he had insisted on treating her to, to the day she set foot in the nature reserve in Costa Rica. Had planned it with her, advised and commented. The truth was, it hadn't felt real. More like they were planning an imaginary journey than a real one, one which would carry Maddie irrevocably away from him, probably for ever. The summer in San Tomo had been a moment out of time, an idyll. Not real life.

Which it was. Wasn't it?

What would have happened if he had dared to look further into his heart on the night of the ball? What if he hadn't made a sudden decision to tell Maddie that thanks to her he was ready to move on, but had taken her on that same walk along the river and told her he loved her and wanted to be with her for ever? What if she had said yes, as she'd indicated she would have? Would he and Arianna have stayed in San Tomo and they all lived happily ever after?

He'd never know.

And knowing he didn't actually believe in happily-ever-after brought him no satisfaction, just an all-consuming suspicion that maybe he was missing out on really living.

The door opened and Arianna mooched in. Dante's heart squeezed at the sight of her. She hadn't been her usual exuberant self since the night of the ball. She wasn't usually one for tears, but she had wept whilst waving her aunt and cousins off, whilst saying goodbye to her *nonna*. The only time she hadn't cried was when they left the *castello* and she had said her *adieu* to Maddie. She had heeded his words, chin up, a proud smile on her lips even as her eyes burned.

Dante wasn't sure exactly what he had said to Maddie or she to him. Commonplace platitudes, no more. She had been back to professional, smooth Madeleine Fitzroy. Gracious and polite to the last, no sign that two days before she had been begging him to tell her that he loved her.

'I'm bored,' Arianna announced.

'Why don't you call one of your friends?'

'They're all still away. No one comes to Rome in August except tourists. If I was in San Tomo I could swim or climb a mountain or play with Flavia or have a sailing lesson or—'

'I get the picture.' Dante cut his daughter off before she listed every single activity in the mountain village.

'Why did we have to come back anyway? You could work there just as easily. Why can't we live there all year round? There's a *scuola primeria* in San Tomo.'

There was. Dante and Luciana had both attended it before moving to the International School in Milan. 'Don't you like living in Rome?'

'Yes, but I'd rather live in San Tomo and ski in winter

and be on the lake all summer. I was happy there—and so were you,' Arianna said with the keen perceptiveness that sometimes surprised him.

'We were on holiday…'

'You were more relaxed. Not as tired.'

'I…' It didn't seem right that his eight-year-old daughter thought him tired and overworked.

'When does Maddie get to New York?'

'Tonight.'

'I wish she wasn't going,' Arianna said in a small voice and Dante pulled her onto his knee.

'You and me both, *bambina*,' he said under his breath.

Arianna turned and snuggled into him, her hair tickling his chin. Dante held her close, protectiveness and love consuming him. 'Papa. Can I tell you something?'

'Anything. Always.'

'I made a wish. In the wishing well at the *castello*.'

'Hmm?'

'I wished for you and Maddie to fall in love. I wanted her to stay and marry you and for you not to be sad any more and for me to have a *mamma*,' Arianna said in a rush.

Dante couldn't speak, holding Arianna tighter as her words sank in. He wasn't just hurting himself, he was hurting Arianna. 'Ari…'

'I really liked Maddie, Papa. Didn't you?'

'*Sì*. I did.'

'Does she know?'

'No,' Dante admitted.

'Why not?'

'It's not always easy to tell someone. You'll learn that one day.'

'That's silly,' Arianna said scornfully. 'If I like someone I'll always tell them, otherwise how will they know?'

'How indeed?'

'You should tell her.'

'I...' Dante stopped. Arianna was right. He should
tell her. Tell her everything he couldn't articulate even
to himself. Find the romance and heart she deserved.
'You're right, Ari. I should tell her. How do you feel
about getting away from Rome for a few days?'

'Sure. Where are we going?'

'New York. Let's go and find Maddie and tell her we
miss her, shall we?'

CHAPTER TWELVE

MADDIE PRACTICALLY LIMPED into the opulent hotel foyer. She wasn't sure she had ever walked so much in her entire life. Sightseeing in Manhattan was, it turned out, excellent practice for walking the Inca Trail. According to her phone, she had been averaging twenty kilometres a day.

She looked at the lifts, just twenty feet away, trying to work out if she had the energy to get to her room. Maybe she needed a little fortifier first. She sank into one of many comfortable loveseats on one side of the foyer, every muscle in her body sighing in relief as the cushions cradled her tired body. If she ever got a place of her own she was going to call this hotel and find out their furniture supplier and order this exact loveseat. And then she would never leave it.

It would be handy if she could also take the service home with her. She had no sooner sat down than one of the neat, friendly waitresses was by her side, smile perfectly in place.

'Good evening, Miss Fitzroy. Did you have a good day?'

'Yes, thank you. I walked down to Brooklyn.'

The waitress's eyes widened. 'Walked?'

'It doesn't look quite so far on a map,' Maddie explained. 'I wanted to explore the Lower East Side and it seemed to make sense to do so on the way down and then walk back up the West Side. I leave tomorrow morning. There's just not enough time to do everything.'

She'd arrived in New York late afternoon two days ago, reasonably alert and refreshed thanks to a First Class upgrade she suspected Dante had paid for. A sweet gesture, but one she couldn't help wishing he hadn't made. She wanted to forget about him, forget about what a fool she had been, forget about the moment she had begged him to love her. Instead every comfortable, pampered moment of her flight she couldn't help thinking how easy it had been for him to treat her. Had it been done as a surprise when he'd paid her bonus, or was it a guilty way of apologising for the way their friendship had come to an abrupt end?

Not that it mattered either way. The only option she had was to carry on with her plans and hope that in time her new experiences would relegate the summer—and Dante—to the back of her mind.

But right now she was still raw; she just refused to allow it to ruin her longed-for trip. She'd spent the first evening wandering around the genteel Upper East Side where her hotel was based before an early dinner in her room. Yesterday she had explored Central Park and the famed Metropolitan Museum before facing the hurly-burly of Times Square and the Theatre District. She'd intended to go and see a show and grab dinner out, but at the last minute she'd retreated to her room and another room service meal in front of the TV. She knew that the next few months would involve many meals alone in strange towns and cities, but she just didn't have the heart to begin yet. There seemed to be happy couples and families everywhere she looked, rubbing in her own lonely state.

Tomorrow she would be more adventurous. She was spending one night in Philadelphia and then a night in Washington and another in Richmond, Virginia, before two nights in Charleston and a further two in Savannah. Her last stop was Florida, where she had a four-night stay before flying down to San Jose. This first two weeks was a way of breaking herself in gently, scheduled trains in a country where she spoke the language. More of a holiday than real travelling.

Once she hit Costa Rica it would all get real. A new language, a different culture. She'd really be on her own. No more five-star hotels like this; she would be bedding down in hostels instead. She might as well make the most of this while she could.

The waitress's soft voice recalled her to her surroundings. 'Can I get you anything, ma'am? A coffee—or maybe a cocktail?'

'A coffee would be lovely. Thank you.'

Maddie sat back in her chair and looked around her. Everyone seemed so put together and confident, as if being surrounded by marble pillars and high, gilt-edged ceilings was commonplace. But they probably thought that about her as well. She always had had the ability to blend in.

She smiled her thanks as the waitress put her coffee in front of her and, for the hundredth time that day, resisted the urge to look at her phone. She was only allowed to do so every two hours. But she could check it every minute and it wouldn't change a thing. Dante wasn't going to get in touch. He had said goodbye to her as coolly and casually as if she were nothing more than the employee she was meant to be. As if his body didn't know every inch of hers. As if they had never confided their deepest fears to each other.

No, she scolded herself. No more. Her time with Dante was done; it was dust. She was moving on into a whole other phase of her life. No longer the obedient Honourable Madeleine, no longer the Runaway Bride, no longer the amenable and helpful Maddie. She wasn't sure who she would be when she finished this experience, but hopefully, like Great-Great-Great-Aunt Ophelia, she would be transformed.

Suffragette, VAD nurse, challenger of primogeniture and all-round badass, Maddie's aunt had lost her lover in World War One, had her bid to inherit Stilling Abbey and the title thrown out of court and, as a result, been ostracised from her outraged family. Undaunted, she had jumped on a boat and explored South America, returning home five years later to become an actress and writer. She was simultaneously the family black sheep and their biggest source of pride. Maddie had been raised on stories of her exploits. It was a photo of Ophelia holding a sloth which had first ignited Maddie's desire to follow in her great-aunt's footsteps. What would she think of her great-niece sitting around and feeling sorry for herself? Not very much. She'd be far more likely to poke her with her parasol and tell her to pull herself together than to offer sympathy.

Tonight, Maddie decided, she wouldn't hide herself away. She would go to a restaurant...she would go to a bar. She might even, feet allowing, go dancing. And she wouldn't think about Dante Falcone once.

Okay. Once, maybe. But no more.

Decision made, she finished her coffee and, wincing at a particularly tender blister, got to her feet. As she did so the waitress came back over, an envelope in her hand. 'Ma'am? This came for you earlier.'

Maddie accepted the envelope in some surprise. Her name was typed on the front. No address. It must have been handed in personally. But she didn't know anyone here, did she? And nobody apart from Dante knew she was here. Her family were aware of her plans to travel, but she hadn't sent them the itinerary yet, meaning to do so from Florida. She knew her mother would consider her whole trip self-indulgent nonsense. She'd been against her leaving England in the first place.

Maddie walked slowly to the lift and, once inside, opened the envelope, pulling out the card within, staring in some puzzlement at the contents. A VIP pass to the Empire State Building for that evening.

'Odd.' No name, no explanation. She had mentioned to the receptionist that morning that she was hoping to go up the iconic tower before her train left in the morning. Maybe they had purchased the ticket for her?

She turned the ticket over. It was date stamped for eight p.m., two hours from now. And hadn't she been intending to go out tonight, tempting as room service and another night curled up in her suite was? This was a sign. She was in the city that allegedly never slept; she really should experience it after dark.

The lift doors opened and Maddie stepped onto the plushly decorated landing. Dante had booked and paid for the hotel, before the ball and the ending of their relationship. It was a far fancier hotel than Maddie, who when in London always stayed at her mother's club with its single beds and boarding-school air, had ever experienced. Her stay was made even more luxurious when she discovered that she had been upgraded to a suite with a gorgeous sitting room with views over Central Park, a bathroom larger than her bedroom at home, complete with a bath big enough for two and a walk-in shower that would probably manage an entire rugby team.

It was incredible, but a little big for one. She felt lost in the huge bed, lonely.

Maddie opened the door and stepped into the suite. Fresh flowers had replaced the still blooming bouquet on the dining table. Fresh wine and chocolates sat on the sideboard and a jug of iced water was ready for her, as if they had timed her return exactly. She really should text Dante and thank him for both the suite and the flight upgrade but she couldn't bring herself to make contact. If he'd booked them after the ball then it was almost as if he was buying her off. He probably wouldn't see it that way, but she couldn't help but think of it as a way to easily assuage his conscience.

She would text him from Costa Rica, she decided. A breezy picture of a sloth with thanks thrown in. And that would be that.

Maddie spent a good hour soaking in the bathtub, watching a TV show as she did so, letting her tired feet recover from their exertions. It didn't take her very long to decide what to wear—carrying her clothes with her for the next four months meant she was travelling light. A couple of pairs of shorts, one pair of lightweight walking trousers, several vest tops and two light hoodies, her bikini, one cotton sundress and one silky dress in case of a more formal occasion. Everything crease-resistant and quick-dry. She wasn't sure her Aunt Ophelia would have approved. She was always incredibly elegant, even when halfway down the Amazon.

Maddie opted for her silky dress and a wrap in case of over-enthusiastic air-conditioning and slipped her feet into her flip-flops. Tonight was good practice for the rest of her trip. No fear, no regrets.

To Maddie's surprise a car was waiting for her. Not a yellow cab, but a sleek, black luxury affair with leather seats and darkened windows. She felt a little like a film star as the driver handed her into the back seat and the car purred quietly through the manic Manhattan traffic. When she got to the famous Art Deco building the driver handed her out and another uniformed man took over, ushering her through the security checks, past the queues of waiting people straight into a lift, then another and then, to her surprise, a third smaller lift.

'Welcome to the one-hundred-and-second floor, ma'am,' the man said as the doors opened and he gestured to her to step out.

The lift opened out, not onto the iconic wraparound balcony she was expecting, but into a room with windows all around, each with a dizzying view of the city. The room was almost empty, just one figure standing at the far end, looking out at the view.

Maddie turned. 'I think there's been...' but the lift doors had already closed. How awkward! She was alone in the room with a stranger.

Only he wasn't a stranger.

He didn't need to turn round for her to recognise him. She knew that stance anywhere. It was Dante.

The lift doors had closed and Dante knew he had just ten minutes. It was highly irregular. The Empire State

Building didn't offer private viewings. However, Dante had contacts who had contacts and somehow a miracle had occurred. He had ten minutes.

Which meant he really had to turn and speak.

He just hoped he found the right words. Remembered the right words.

Slowly he turned round. Maddie stood by the doors, staring at him as if he was the ghost of mistakes past. His heart stuttered as he drank in the sight of her, tall and elegant as ever in a long blue dress, her hair pinned up. Only the vulnerability and uncertainty in her eyes was new.

'Ciao.'

Not a great start, but not too terrible either. You couldn't go too wrong with a simple greeting.

'Dante? What on earth are you doing here?'

'We missed you,' he said simply.

'But why the elaborate set-up? You knew where I was staying. Or you could have called…'

'Heart and romance. You wanted heart and romance.'

Understanding flared in her eyes, followed by hope before she wiped all expression off her face. 'Yes. I did.'

Dante took a deep breath. Either he was about to make a colossal fool of himself or… '"Arise, fair sun, and kill the envious moon, Who is already sick and pale with grief That thou, her maid, art far more fair than she."'

Maddie just stared. At least she hadn't laughed. Emboldened, he took a step forward and then another until he was close enough to touch. '"Did my heart love till now?"' Was that his voice, so husky? '"Forswear it, sight! For I ne'er saw true beauty till this night."'

'Dante…'

'Maddie.' With relief he abandoned the carefully rehearsed lines from *Romeo and Juliet*. 'I am a fool. I refused to listen to what my heart was saying. It was so wrong in the past I didn't dare trust that this time it could be right. I told myself the best thing I could do was to let you go. To plan a life without you in it.'

'Dante…' she said again, but he ploughed on. If he didn't speak now he never would. 'When you left, I told myself that it was for the best. That you deserved more, that I didn't deserve anything. But the truth is I was too afraid to try. Too afraid to get it wrong again. Too afraid that I might let you down.'

Her mouth wobbled. 'You could only let me down by not trying.'

'Ti amo,' he said huskily. 'I love you and I want the whole world to know it. I know I might be too late. I know I probably have lost your respect. That evening by the lake you asked me to love you. You shouldn't have needed to ask—I should have proclaimed it to the whole ball. I hadn't dared admit my feelings to myself—although it seems that my sister and daughter both knew more about how I felt about you than I did. I would have been lying to you if I had spoken then. But I can tell you tonight, in absolute truth, that I love you and if one day you would consider marrying me then I will spend my life proving to you that you did the right thing.'

Was she hallucinating? Was she really standing in a glass room one hundred floors up listening to Dante Falcone proclaim his love for her? Maddie reached out and ran her hand down the dear remembered planes of his face, the warmth of his skin proof that he was really here, not a figment of her overtired imagination. 'I can't believe you're here.'

'Arianna and I arrived yesterday. She's back at the hotel with a sitter,' he added. 'She's part of me. The best part of me. We come as a team, so it felt right she came too.'

'She's here? But I leave tomorrow!'

'I know.' His smile was tender and Maddie curled her hand around his cheek, unable to let go, convinced that if she stopped touching him he would disappear. 'I helped plan this trip, remember? I know every place, every stop. So,' now he looked unsure, as unsure as she had ever seen him, 'if you would allow two gatecrashers then Ari and I would love to accompany you to Florida, where she is planning to go on every roller coaster in the state. If you would rather travel alone then we understand. In that case we will fly to Florida and Ari's plans still stand. And I...' His voice trailed off. 'I will wish you all the love and luck in the world.'

Maddie's heart was so full of joy and hope it ached with a sweetness entirely new to her. Her lonely trip would no longer be lonely. Dante wanted to be with her; Ari was here. No tables for one and long nights trying to convince herself she was having fun. 'I'm sure there's room for two extra passengers,' she said, wondering why he wasn't touching her yet. Couldn't he see that she was trembling with need? 'Just to Florida?'

'After Ari has made herself suitably scared we need to go home. I am planning to sell the Rome house and move back to the *castello*. But I think you should carry on with your plans. I don't want to step in your way.'

Maddie could feel tears burning in her eyes. 'Plans can change,' she said. 'If a better offer comes along.'

'I'm not sure it's better, but it's all I have, Maddie.' Finally, finally he had taken her hands in his, his touch igniting a fire within her she never wanted to burn out. Maddie stared up at Dante, drinking in the austere lines of his face, quivering at the heat and passion burning in his eyes. How could she ever have thought this man a cold statue?

'Madeleine Fitzroy. *Ti amo. Vuoi sposarmi?* I love you. Will you do me the greatest honour and become my Contessa, my wife?'

Yes! her heart shouted, but she stilled it. 'On one condition.'

'Anything,' he promised, his heart in his eyes, and Maddie held tightly on to his hands, unable to believe that all that love, that desire was for her.

'I still want to see sloths…' she said, her mouth curving into a provocative smile. 'What do you think about honeymooning in Costa Rica?'

'If you marry me I will happily spend my honeymoon with mould-covered bears, anywhere you desire. Maddie, I know how much time you have spent planning and looking forward to this trip. Are you sure you want to cancel?'

'Postpone,' she said. 'I still intend to go to every single country on my list, but I don't have to do it all at once. I'd rather go with someone by my side, share my adventures with someone. If you'll come.'

'With you? Anywhere,' he vowed and then slowly, with infinite tenderness he kissed her as if it was the first time, a gentle caress filled with more love than Maddie had ever thought possible. She leaned in to the kiss, holding him tight, never wanting to let him go. He had her heart, her soul and she knew that she had his. It was all she had ever wanted. She'd wanted adventure, to discover who she was. Maddie knew that her greatest adventures were about to start and that Dante Falcone would be by her side the entire time.

EPILOGUE

She'd been here before. A white dress. A bunch of flowers. An expectant groom. Last time she had been on the verge of being a Countess; this time she was planning on becoming a *contessa*. But the title didn't matter. The castle didn't matter. All that mattered was the man waiting for her and the small girl by her side.

'This is so romantic,' Arianna said, looking around at the other wedding groups in the foyer, all waiting for their number to be called, waiting for the moment they were finally married. 'When I grow up I want to do exactly the same.'

Maddie put an arm around her and held her close. 'When you grow up I think your father will hope you got married at the *castello*, but the truth is, Ari, it's not the wedding that's important, it's being married. It's not the setting. It's the vows you make and meaning them.'

Last time Maddie had planned a huge society wedding. The type that meant she had existed on no carbs and excessive exercise to make sure the slim-fitting designer dress had hung on her perfectly, the type where every family member, no matter how far removed, had been invited. A wedding that had required a team of wedding planners and had nearly induced a nervous breakdown in her mother when the napkins hadn't quite matched the tablecloths. She didn't want that again. Nor did she want any Runaway Bride headlines. She just wanted to marry Dante.

So here they were, still in New York, waiting in line at City Hall for a quick and simple wedding. They'd only had to give twenty-four hours' notice after registering for their licence and she and Arianna had spent the time shopping for a simple white dress for Maddie and a matching silver one for Arianna, before heading to a spa for facials and haircuts and mani-pedis. It was a far cry from her last hen weekend on the Côte d'Azur, but a lot more enjoyable, spending time with the serious girl who was going to be her new daughter. They had already decided that there would be no 'steps' in their family. And maybe riding roller coasters in Florida wasn't Maddie's first choice of honeymoon destination, but they had promised Arianna a week of fun before her au pair arrived to take her back to the *castello* and prepare her for school, while Dante and Maddie headed down to Costa Rica for a fortnight alone. Dante had drawn the line at hostels, but, as he had booked them a gorgeous villa right on the beach, Maddie decided she would allow him his way this time.

'Nervous?' Arianna whispered as the sweet couple in vintage dress who had been waiting next to them got up and walked into the chapel. Maddie's chest squeezed. They were next.

'Not at all. I'm just excited.'

'The only thing we need to be nervous about is telling Zia Luciana and Nonna that we got married at City Hall and they weren't invited,' Dante said, smiling at

Maddie with the sudden sweet smile she had fallen for just a few weeks ago.

'But as we will celebrate with them all in New Zealand at Christmas, and I will let my parents organise their own party for us, I think we'll be forgiven,' Maddie reassured her.

And then it was their turn. The three of them and a photographer who would act as a witness as well as recording the moment Maddie gave herself to Dante and he to her. The short ceremony passed in a blur. All Maddie knew was the intensity and love in Dante's eyes as he recited his vows, the feeling of rightness as she said hers, the sheer happiness when the clerk pronounced them married, the joy in Arianna's face as she hugged her new mother and the moment Dante took her hand and promised her huskily that he would never let her down.

It was all she needed to know. It wasn't the wedding… it was the marriage. And she was more than ready. The Runaway Bride had stopped running. She'd found her family at last.

* * * * *

LET'S TALK
Romance

For exclusive extracts, competitions and special offers, find us online:

- f facebook.com/millsandboon
- ⊙ @millsandboonuk
- 🐦 @millsandboon

Or get in touch on 0844 844 1351*

For all the latest titles coming soon, visit millsandboon.co.uk/nextmonth

*Calls cost 7p per minute plus your phone company's price per minute access charge

Want even more
ROMANCE?

Join our bookclub today!

'Mills & Boon books, the perfect way to escape for an hour or so.'

Miss W. Dyer

'Excellent service, promptly delivered and very good subscription choices.'

Miss A. Pearson

'You get fantastic special offers and the chance to get books before they hit the shops'

Mrs V. Hall

Visit millsandbook.co.uk/Bookclub and save on brand new books.

MILLS & BOON